NEW BLOOD

CHAINS OF COMMAND BOOK 1

ZEN DIPIETRO

PARALLEL WORLDS PRESS

COPYRIGHT

COPYRIGHT © 2018 BY ZEN DIPIETRO

This is a work of fiction. Names, characters, organizations, events, and incidents are either products of the author's imagination or used fictitiously. Any resemblance to actual events, business establishments, locales, or persons, living or dead, is coincidental.

All rights reserved. No part of this publication may be reproduced, stored in a retrieval system, or transmitted in any form or by any means (electronic, mechanical, photocopying, recording, or otherwise) without express written permission of the publisher. The only exception is brief quotations for the purpose of review.

Please purchase only authorized electronic editions. Distribution of this book via the Internet or via any other means without the permission of the publisher is illegal and punishable by law.

ISBN: 978-1-943931-23-1 (print)

Published in the United States of America by Parallel Worlds Press

DRAGONFIRE STATION UNIVERSE

Original Series (complete)
Dragonfire Station Book 1: Translucid
Dragonfire Station Book 2: Fragments
Dragonfire Station Book 3: Coalescence

Intersections (Dragonfire Station Short Stories)

Mercenary Warfare series (complete)
Selling Out
Blood Money
Hell to Pay
Calculated Risk
Going for Broke

Chains of Command
New Blood
Blood and Bone
Cut to the Bone
Out for Blood

To get updates on releases and sales, sign up for Zen's newsletter.

1

Emiko arrived on campus at the PAC Academy knowing she was different than the other students.

At only sixteen years of age, she was among the youngest accepted. That wasn't what set her apart, though.

Being an overachiever was nothing special there, either. Most people with high aspirations in any field of study went to the PAC Academy.

The thing that made Emiko different was that she was a brand-new person. Literally. While other students arrived on campus as the person they had always been from birth, she'd been assigned a whole new identity.

An identity with a purpose. If she succeeded at the academy and continued on her intended path of becoming a clandestine operations agent, there would be no way to trace her past and use her family against her. A new identity was a necessary precaution for the safety of the officer, the family, and the PAC itself.

No, not *if*. She *would* succeed. Failure was unacceptable. She would not wash out. She would put everything she had into her work to be the best.

She would get accepted into officer training school.

She would become a clandestine operations intelligence officer.

There was no other acceptable outcome. She'd already spent years working toward it, ever since her father had explained to her what special ops meant. She'd known that was what she was meant to do. There was no backup plan. Nothing else would be acceptable.

"Emiko Arashi." She practiced the name, letting the sounds roll over her tongue. "Hello, I'm Emiko."

As she repeated the words over and over, trying to break them in like a pair of new shoes, she unpacked her bags. At least she had a dorm room to herself. She had little in common with most people her age, and doubted she'd have made a good roommate to the typical new student at the Planetary Alliance Cooperative Academy.

She set her suitcase on the narrow bed and opened it. There wasn't much inside. She'd packed several outfits and toiletries. That was about it, besides her favorite weapons. She needed little else.

Everything but her sword and bo staff fit into the dresser alongside the bed.

There. All moved in. She had two hours to kill, though, before the orientation meeting.

Besides the bed and the dresser, her small room had a desk and a tiny closet. She wouldn't really need the closet until she earned a uniform, hopefully in the third and final year of the academy. She might hang a chin-up bar in it so she could work out in her room during study breaks.

When she opened the door to peek inside, she laughed when she saw a bar already spanning the width of the closet. Some previous occupant had had the same idea. Probably also an ambitious student who'd been aiming for officer training school—or OTS, as it was more commonly known.

She wondered if that student had been accepted.

She closed the closet. Her knife collection, sword, and bo would fit nicely in there.

The chair tucked against the desk didn't look comfortable. She sat and her suspicion was confirmed. She'd need to do something about that. With all the hours she'd put in at this desk, she'd need a place to sit that wouldn't make her back ache.

When she touched the voicecom display, it came to life. She sent a quick message to her parents to let them know she'd arrived and was settling in. She had brought no holo-images of them or her brother, or anything else that would tie her to her life back home or her parents' little house just outside of Tokyo. Surely she wouldn't need them, anyway. Her family was only a few hours away and she'd visit them during breaks.

She'd miss her family, but she'd still be better off than the students who wouldn't see their parents for years because they lived on another planet within the Planetary Alliance Cooperative. Compared to that, she had it easy.

Her parents had always been supportive of her, even when she didn't fit in easily because of her narrow focus on her academic studies and her martial arts skills. She hadn't been ostracized, but she hadn't been popular, either. Her parents had never suggested she be more like the other kids. They understood her, and for good reason. Her father was a captain with central intelligence, and her mother was a commander in the diplomatic corps.

Serving the Alliance ran in her blood. Even her older brother had gotten into the business, studying to be a civil engineer to help cities operate efficiently.

She caught her train of thought and stopped it in its tracks. While she was at the academy, she was not their daughter. She was not Kano's sister. She'd been recruited as a clandestine ops hopeful, and as such, she had two sets of records: one official set, with birth name and information, and a second set of real records to go with the new identity. The records with her birth name would reflect a fictionalized account of her life, should anyone bother to look her up. The records for her new identity would reflect her actual career with the PAC.

The new version of her would become the real her. She needed to get accustomed to thinking of herself as Emiko so that when she met people, she could immediately respond with Emiko's fabricated personal details.

It would take some getting used to.

With nothing else to do, she configured the voicecom the way she liked it, with her calendar, messages, and favorite academic resources all arranged in a tidy row along the right side.

She still had an hour and forty-five minutes before the orientation.

"I should probably go and see if any of my neighbors have arrived." She remained seated for a long moment. Sighing, she stood.

She'd never had much luck fitting in with the crowd. She'd had a few good friends at her school, and more that she was friendly enough with, but for the most part, she'd found her peers to be aimless and undisciplined. Given that about half of her academy classmates had no intentions of going on to OTS to become officers, there would probably be a fair bit of youthful foolishness here as well.

At least some of those students would be from other planets. That should give her a chance to practice her language and communication skills.

She turned her attention to the voices echoing down the hall. They were distorted enough that she couldn't make out the words, but the enthusiasm of two distinct voices was unmistakable. It seemed her neighbors were indeed moving in that day, too.

She smoothed her fingers over her fine, black hair, gathered into a thin ponytail. She straightened her PAC-issued t-shirt and cargo pants, then set her jaw.

"Okay. Let's do this."

Her first undercover assignment would be to assume the role of a typical academy student. As she walked across the hall and down a few meters, she got into character, adopting a soft, friendly smile and wide eyes.

A door stood open. A pair of young women sat with their heads bent over a comport. No one was talking, though, so they obviously weren't in the middle of a call. Emiko knocked on the doorframe, peering in.

Two heads turned, revealing her neighbors to be a human and a Bennite. Emiko found that interesting. Bennaris was devoted almost entirely to the medical profession, which they tended to dominate. Few Bennites attended the academy.

"Hi!" chirped the human with short blond hair. She bounced up to her feet and executed the polite bow of one PAC student to another.

The Bennite smiled and stood to bow. Her tanned skin complemented her dark hair and eyes. Emiko returned the bow in equal measure.

"Did you just arrive?" the blond asked. "I'm Jane."

Was she really? Emiko wondered. Not that it was likely that the first person she met on campus was another covert ops hopeful. Very few, if any, were recruited each year. Nonetheless, she had to remember that not everyone around her would be who they seemed to be.

It would be part of her education.

"I'm Val," the Bennite said.

"Emiko."

Both of her neighbors were prettier than her. Emiko had average Japanese looks. Black hair, dark eyes, and a heart-shaped face. Nice enough, but also entirely forgettable. Not that she cared about her looks. Unlike these girls, she didn't bother with cosmetics. She only wished to be clean and healthy, with a tidy appearance.

Jane had a fresh-faced girl next door look, with a sprinkling of freckles over the bridge of her nose and her cheeks. Val had a more sophisticated look—youthful, but polished.

"Did you just get in?" Val asked.

"Yes, a bit ago. Are you going to the orientation?"

Jane shook her head. "We went to the one last night. We got in early yesterday, but went out to get some things for the room to make it a bit more homey."

"Did you already know each other?" Emiko asked.

Her neighbors nodded.

"We met about a year ago at a medical career expo. We're both studying to be doctors," Jane said.

Emiko nodded. "Officers?"

"We hope so," Val said. "If not, we'll still have the best pre-med education possible, and be qualified to work at PAC facilities."

"What are you studying?" Val asked.

"Security, with a pilot rating." Emiko wasn't lying. She simply wasn't telling the entire truth.

"Piloting! That sounds fun." Jane's eyes sparkled.

Emiko nodded, smiling. She didn't volunteer that she was already rated to pilot a PAC shuttle. She'd been working on her flying skills for years. But she wanted to fly big ships, too. The faster and more powerful, the better.

"Sounds like you'll have some intensive training classes," Val said thoughtfully.

"I'm looking forward to it." Emiko couldn't have meant it more. She couldn't wait to get started.

"Well, it's good to meet you," Jane said. "We look forward to getting to know you."

Emiko was relieved that Jane had so adeptly given her an out. For a first meeting, this had been pleasant. She wasn't great at small talk, but hopefully she could get to know her neighbors organically. Maybe while taking part in campus activities.

She gave them a polite bow and excused herself. It was too

early to go to the orientation, but she didn't want to go back to her room and sit. A walk around the campus seemed like a good idea. She already had the map memorized. Some people called her ability "photographic" or "eidetic" memory, but those were both inaccurate terms. She preferred to think of it of it simply as an ability to retain most of what she learned. She rarely forgot things.

Seeing the campus with her own eyes would be different, though, and familiarizing herself with her new home would be a productive use of her time.

She started by making a circuit around her dorm, noting the locations of all the windows and doors, the paths, and the lighting. Then she followed the path that created a circuit of similar dormitory buildings, all along the perimeter of the campus. Within that roughly circular shape, the other buildings resided.

The campus had been thoughtfully designed, with plenty of trees and wide spaces for gathering. Benches and grassy areas practically begged for a student to settle in with an infoboard and a comport to get work done while enjoying sunshine and fresh air. She could imagine herself doing a fair amount of studying outdoors.

A large area in the center of campus lay adjacent to the majority of the classrooms. Beautiful landscaping and trees that lined the outer walkway made it remarkably inviting. She could imagine groups of students out there, playing impromptu games of jump ball or throwing a disk back and forth. She looked forward to settling against a tree to read in between classes.

She spent her remaining time leading up to the orientation committing every path, tree, and building to memory. Tomorrow, she'd begin casing each building.

Her father and her training had taught her a lot about being aware of her surroundings, and taking every advantage she could get. She liked to think that this knowledge would give her an edge over other intelligence candidates.

But then, perhaps they had backgrounds that eclipsed hers. There was no way to know. She'd just have to give everything she had to her studies, to make sure she succeeded.

The orientation hall yawned large all around Emiko. She took a seat near the back and settled in, watching her fellow classmates.

Her competition.

She'd known most of the students would be older. Sixteen was young to begin the academy, and most of the faces she saw of the incoming students looked to be eighteen or nineteen.

Emiko had put a lot of effort into not being average and meeting the application requirements early. She hadn't taken summers off or wasted time on dating.

She had a goal, and only that goal had mattered.

While waiting for the dean to speak, she observed her competition. There would be four orientation sessions like this, with about five hundred people attending each. It was a decent enough cross-section. Since most of her classmates were older, they largely displayed proper maturity for the occasion. She didn't see many students doing youthful, foolish things like clowning around with friends. This was the academy. Even the least-dedicated among them would feel the gravity of that.

The grouping was diverse enough that she couldn't discern much about it as a whole. A shame. She liked to have as much information as possible about her rivals. She'd have to keep an eye out for those whose performance rose above the others.

"Welcome to the Planetary Alliance Cooperative Academy," the dean began.

Emiko focused her attention on him. He was a middle-aged human with gray hair, and in good shape.

"If you don't already know, I'm Rob Delinger, Dean of the PAC academy. It's a great pleasure to look out on all these faces, representing so many species and cultures. That's what the PAC is all about. We hope that in coming together in the spirit of cooperation and mutual betterment, we can all become more than the sum of our parts."

The dean, projected on a screen for those in the back to see, smiled. "You're probably expecting me to say something about looking to your left and to your right, and about how a bunch of you won't make it through. I don't do those speeches. For those who don't make it through their three years here, I like to think that they've learned invaluable things that they'll keep with them for the rest of their lives. Yes, some of you will leave before the first semester is over. And more will go before the second year begins. But those of you who make it through your third year will have received one of the finest educations in this galaxy. And some of you will even become officers. Who knows—maybe one of you in this room will eventually become the dean of this academy. You are all at the edge of possibility right now, and all you have to do is work your hardest to achieve your dreams."

A murmur went through the assemblage. This was a more chipper speech than incoming students, including Emiko, had expected. She'd been prepared for a very militant welcome. This touchy-feely approach felt different. Welcoming.

Interesting. Her opinion of Dean Delinger went up.

Some would say that, as a default, her opinion of the dean should be high. Emiko didn't work that way. Every person she came across, regardless of how she behaved in their presence, had to earn her respect.

Delinger had gotten a decent start.

He turned his head to look out at the crowd, and a spotlight made the gray in his hair turn silvery. "All of you in this room will study the cornerstones of the PAC. You'll learn about the governments of PAC member-planets and trade allies. You'll learn governmental policies and procedures. Interspecies relations.

And the regular complement of sciences, technologies, and mathematics. And you'll learn your specialties, too. Languages, medicine, piloting, engineering, database and file management, and diplomacy, to mention just a few. Regardless of your long-term goals, your education here will be the bedrock of the rest of your life."

Emiko smiled. Finally, her life was beginning. She'd been in a holding pattern until this very moment.

"So, welcome to the academy. You'll make friendships here that will last your entire life. You'll learn things that you will always remember. And if you work hard, you just might become great."

He said this last with a tilt of his head that elicited a laugh from the students. Not that it was a great joke, but everyone there wanted to become great and the possibility struck home.

Emiko sat through introductions to the prominent members of the faculty, but she was only taking notes for future reference. It mattered little to her what these people said. What mattered was how well they taught and how much they knew. Some weren't professors she'd ever take classes with, anyway.

The rest of the speeches were motivational, cautionary, and otherwise meant for people who weren't Emiko. She didn't need all that. She already knew what she needed to do. It was just a matter of the details involved with getting it done.

She slipped out near the end, when the auxiliary services department was explaining the medical and mental health care offered, and that students shouldn't hesitate to take advantage of those options.

Other than possibly getting injured during physical training, she wouldn't be needing those services. She was healthy and had her head on straight.

As she took a circuitous route back to her dorm, she decided that her first mission as an academy student was to appear to be one of them. Fitting in would be her cover identity.

Emiko Arashi would be well-rounded, friendly, and not stick out.

Just a regular sixteen-year-old studying hard.

As part of the yearly kickoff, the academy hosted a clubs and activities mixer on the quad. Emiko had been on campus for three days, and with classes not starting for another week, she was glad for something to focus her energy on.

She wasn't much of a joiner, and expected to spend most of her time studying, but Val and Jane bubbled with excitement at the opportunity of joining campus life. Therefore, Emiko put on her just-like-everyone-else face and went with them to see what campus life had to offer. Just like a typical student would.

"Check out the guy at the holo-vid club," Jane hissed under her breath so the student in question wouldn't hear her. "With the yellow shirt."

Casually, Val and Emiko looked. He was cute, with curly brown hair that hung over his forehead and smiling brown eyes.

"Is he Zerellian?" Val asked. "I have a hard time telling Zerellian humans and Earth humans apart."

"Wow," Emiko said, her voice full of surprise. "That's a really species-ist thing to say."

Val's dark eyes widened in a stricken expression. "It is? I'm so sorry…I didn't mean it as a bad thing. Just that I'm still too ignorant to distinguish. Please accept my apologies. The deficiency is entirely mine."

She bowed at the waist, deeply enough to convey respect and repentance.

Jane and Emiko laughed.

"She's kidding," Jane said. "We often can't tell the difference either. A person's accent or clothing style can give clues, but we usually just have to guess."

"Sorry." Emiko grinned. "I couldn't resist the chance to tease you."

Val laughed. "I should probably be mad, but I'm just glad I didn't say something insulting. I see I'm going to have to be careful around you."

Val shook an admonishing finger at Emiko, chuckling.

Emiko had never been known for teasing or joking, but she supposed that would give her a more easygoing persona, compared to the reputation of a no-nonsense, serious student she had back home.

It would be more fun, too, and more likely to attract friends.

"Let's go check it out," Jane said, her eyes still on the curly haired guy. "I love holo-vids. It would be fun to watch them with big groups of other students."

"You go ahead," Val answered. "I want to check out the archery club."

"You don't do archery." Jane looked puzzled.

"I know, but I've always been interested. Maybe I could learn. I don't watch many holo-vids." She smiled apologetically.

"Okay." Jane looked to Emiko as Val strode away. "You like holo-vids, right?"

"Definitely." As far as Emiko was concerned, a holo-vid club seemed like an easy way to take part in something without having to expend much time or effort. And she loved a good action vid.

The curly haired guy lit up when they approached, and he launched into an enthusiastic explanation of the kinds of movies the club watched, how often they met up, and so forth. He included Emiko in the conversation, though it was clear that he was far more interested in Jane.

After a few minutes, Emiko started to feel superfluous. She excused herself to do some looking around.

"Will you come watch with us next week?" the guy asked.

"Sure, if Jane does," Emiko agreed. Judging by Jane's rapt expression, she was pretty sure that they'd be in attendance.

She walked among the tables that had been set up to advertise the fun of outdoor sports groups or the learning experiences of the various clubs. Nothing in particular drew her attention, but it was nice to see her classmates interacting casually. She felt like she had more in common with these people than she ever had with people her own age back home. She saw a light in them. A determination to succeed, mixed up with ambition and hope for the future. It reminded her of herself.

The realization made her optimistic. Maybe fitting in wouldn't require great effort. Maybe she could relax, be herself, and actually enjoy things.

A loud noise behind her caused her to spin around with her fists up and drop her body into a fighting stance. She searched the gathering, looking for a threat, then saw that someone had dropped a large wooden board on top of another. Some sort of game setup, from the look of it.

She let her hands drop and adopted a casual posture. Everyone else had been startled as well, and no one seemed to have noticed her reaction.

She'd have to work on that.

As she moved on, she reminded herself not to take the safety of campus life for granted. She had to keep her guard up. Not so much that she seemed strange, but fitting in couldn't distract her from long-term goals.

She'd have to work on finding a balance between the two, as well.

Classes hadn't even started, and she already had a lot to work on.

Emiko spotted Val near the language club table and dodged around a few people to join her.

"Do you like languages?" Emiko asked.

Val nodded. "I'm fluent in Standard and Bennite, but I'd like to learn more. I will, in classes, but it would be helpful to have people to practice with. Do you speak anything besides Standard?"

"No," Emiko lied. "My parents didn't even speak Japanese at home."

"That's a shame," Val said, her eyes full of kindness and understanding. "But lots of people only speak Standard. And you can always learn if you want to."

Emiko nodded. "I've always meant to give it a try, but haven't found the time."

In truth, she spoke six languages as fluently as a native, and was actively learning more. That ability didn't fit with her cover identity, though, so she would keep it a secret.

"Did you find any activities that sounded fun to you?" Val asked brightly. She seemed to have a mothering quality that Emiko found endearing.

"Jane and I are going to try out the holo-vid club. I also noticed a food club that learns about and tries foods from planets in the PAC zone. That sounds really interesting." Emiko figured that, in her future travels, she'd have to rely a great deal on whatever a planet happened to offer. She'd be well-served to know about those cuisines. Plus, any club that was all about eating good food sounded great to her.

"That does sound neat," Val agreed. "Let's go take a look."

WHEN THE HOLO-VID club's first meeting rolled around, Emiko and Jane enjoyed a showing of a classic detective vid. When the dining club met, she and Val learned about Kanaran food. The outings were simple and fun, and cemented her relationship with her two new friends. She appreciated their positive attitudes and thoughtfulness. Considering how differently the roommate situation could have gone, Emiko had gotten extremely lucky.

Not so with her neighbors on the other side of the hall, who'd turned out to be argumentative and spiteful. Once classes began, Emiko quickly learned how to avoid crossing paths with them.

As she dug into the coursework, she worked at striking the right balance between the obsessive study that came naturally to her and maintaining her cover identity. She didn't always succeed. Sometimes she did too much of one, only to overcompensate by doing too much of the other.

The academy took schoolwork to a new level, even for her. In spite of the difficulty it posed in maintaining a normal social life, she reveled in the rigorous classes and the competition her classmates provided. She'd definitely gone from being a standout in a small place to being one of many achievers in a large place. She loved the change.

Though not a math major, as a pilot, she had to take a great deal of math and physics to understand the nature of spaceflight. She wished she'd get some flying time in the near future, but first she'd have to work through flight theory, mechanics, and endless hours in simulators.

One thing at a time.

After two months of study, she felt entirely at home, having settled into a comfortable, though, challenging routine.

She was, by all of her own measures, doing great.

She hadn't made it to all the holo-vid club meetings, but the fifth one featured an action vid she wanted to see. It wasn't new, but she'd never gotten around to watching it, and since she hadn't attended the last meeting, this one would be perfect for her. She'd consider it her reward for getting the top mark on her first academy math exam. There was always another exam around the corner, though, so she spent her afternoon studying.

Jane's knock at the door of Emiko's dorm surprised her. Three hours had passed already? Emiko put her infoboard aside, grabbed her hooded sweatshirt, and greeted her friend.

"Ready for some action?" Jane asked.

Emiko pulled the sweatshirt over her head, knocking her

ponytail askew. She pulled it loose, then regathered it neatly. "Yes, but be careful. Someone overhearing that might get the wrong idea."

Jane laughed and bumped her with an elbow as they set off for the Campbell Hall, which had a large seating area and the setup to accommodate group viewings.

They exchanged some waves with people who had arrived before them, and took seats near a few people they'd become friendly with in the club. Shortly thereafter, the lights dimmed and the vid started.

Emiko enjoyed the movie, the snacks, and the hour of discussion that always followed a showing. By the time she got back to her dorm, she was tired but happy. The next day would be busy, and a little recreation time was a good way to hone her focus.

Her bedtime routine had become that of a shower, brushing her teeth, and falling into bed, exhausted. There never seemed to be enough hours in the day, but the fatigue served her well by ensuring that she never suffered from insomnia.

EMIKO AWOKE blind and unable to move.

Stifling her confusion and panic, she used her senses to discover what she could. Pressure on her stomach and chest made breathing difficult and she became lightheaded. The air around her was hot and muggy. A small, regular motion rocked her slightly from beneath, back and forth.

Her head was either inside a bag or wrapped up in a blanket. Possibly her whole body had been, as well. Flexing her fingers, she felt taut fabric. Too taut to be a bag. When she tightened her grip, she felt the give of someone else's flesh.

Okay, she was being carried over someone's shoulder with a bag over her head. She wasn't being handled roughly, though it was hard to breathe and she had a shoulder crammed into her stomach. Each passing moment increased the discomfort, and every footstep her abductor took caused a slight jarring that increased the ache in her stomach. There was nothing she could do at the moment, though. She'd have to conserve her strength for when she had an opportunity to fight.

What felt like several minutes later, strong arms swung her down and set her upright in a chair. A touch around her neck warned her what was coming just a moment before a shaft of light pierced her optic nerve, blinding her.

Squinting and taking deep breaths of fresh air as her eyes adjusted, she looked for her abductor.

Her captor must have slipped out the door while she was unable to see. She hadn't heard anything.

She was alone in a room empty of anything but the chair she sat in. Her eyes were adjusting, and she examined every detail around her.

Escape would be impossible, she was certain. But gathering information about her surroundings was all she could do. She examined the door and found it to have a locking mechanism she couldn't get past.

She ran her hands over each of the four walls, tapping them in places to determine their depth and strength. Then she pried up a piece of loose tile to examine the subflooring. Concrete. No help there.

Fine. She'd wait. She returned to the chair.

She had no way of knowing how much time had gone by, but she'd have guessed that the better part of an hour passed before the door opened.

She remained seated as a tall human walked in wearing nondescript black pants and a shirt.

He was thirtyish with dark, streaky blond hair pulled back in a tiny ponytail. He was good-looking enough to be interesting, but not to the extent that his looks were a defining characteristic for him.

"Do you know who I am?" he asked.

"No."

"Do you know why you're here?"

Again, she said, "No."

"What if I said you had to fight me to get out of this room?"

"I'd say let's go." She stayed where she was.

He grinned, looking rakish and roguish and everything else that landed just short of debauchery. It made her want to like him, in spite of her circumstances.

"Hi, Emiko. I'm Ross Whelkin, and I'll be your hand-to-hand combat teacher."

"Do you always introduce yourself this way?" She fought not to let the extent of her annoyance and anxiety show, but her heart still hadn't settled down to a normal pace.

He laughed. "Only with brand-new recruits who think they want to get into the game of spies and assassins. Change your mind yet?"

"No"

He leaned casually against the door. "You've been remarkably calm. Maybe you'll be one of the ones that are good at faking. But why don't you tell me what you think this is all about?"

"You should have roughed me up a little if you wanted me to think I was in a life-or-death situation. You were too gentle. And you should have taken me out of the building. I'd guess we're in the service basement of my dorm, because the acoustics around us never changed, and neither did the smell."

He nodded. "So you knew it was a test, then?"

"Yes. I'm not important enough for anyone to bother kidnapping, and a PAC campus would be a tremendously poor choice of place to grab a nobody, given the likelihood of being seen or caught on surveillance."

"Then you've just passed your first test."

"What's the success rate of this test?" she asked.

"Classified. Maybe someday you'll earn your clearance."

"Okay. So what now?"

He shrugged. "Now you can go back to your dorm and get some sleep. Tomorrow, I'll begin your combat training. We'll start with an assessment of your current skills."

She stood. "We're both here. Why wait?"

"This isn't the right place for that."

"If you'd like to lead the way, sir, I'll follow."

He gave her a long, hard look, then grinned. "You're on. Let's go."

AN HOUR LATER, Emiko was sweaty, sore, and riding a wave of adrenaline. Ross Whelkin had slammed her to the mat a dozen times, but each time, she'd learned something new. This was nothing like the training she'd done before, or participating in competitions for trophies and ribbons.

"That's enough," he finally said, and they bowed to each other. "Have a seat."

She brushed a loose strand of hair from her forehead as she did so.

"You have excellent skills for your age. In competition and sparring, no doubt, you'd be among the best students here. However, these private lessons are not about winning titles or medals. They're about incapacitating or killing, and not getting yourself killed. You have a lot to learn. Competition fighting and the real thing only have the very basics in common."

She bowed her head in acknowledgement.

"The general curriculum combat classes are about to begin, and you'll be attending to maintain your cover. You're scheduled for my afternoon class."

"Should I hide my skill level?" she asked.

"No. But don't mention titles you've won, as that's something people could look into. I'm guessing you've won regional titles. Probably more. Am I right?"

Was he pretending he hadn't seen her entire life's history laid out in her records, or had he simply not cared enough to note her accomplishments?

Or did he just want her to think that?

"Five-time regional champion, two-time hemisphere champion." She said it matter-of-factly, without a hint of pride. Here, those titles meant nothing, and she knew that now.

He simply nodded. "Just stick to competition and sparring style in class, with none of the tactics you'll be learning from me privately. Some of the students in that class are aiming to be security officers for real, and they'll work harder if you set a high bar for them. You'll learn a thing or two as well, probably, by watching your classmates and how they apply the lessons."

"I see."

It would seem that the academy had more than one reason for creating her new identity the way they had. She wondered what other things she'd discover as she went along.

"Good. I'll be working with you twice a week outside of your class hours, for now. We can schedule a time that works around your academics."

He opened the door. Apparently, they were done here.

"Anything else?" she asked.

"If your bruises need attention, go to the medical bay and see Doctor Hafli or Doctor Yates. They'll make sure such things don't go into your medical files."

"I'm fine," she lied. From experience, she knew she'd need a couple days.

He gave her a knowing look, but didn't argue. "Other than that, have a good weekend, and I'll see you next week. Oh. One more thing. If you're serious about this, you need to work your ass off, Emiko. There's no halfway in this. If you aren't ready to push yourself to a wall and then through the wall, you might as well take back your birth identity and become a real security officer."

She hardened her expression to avoid scowling at him. "I'll go through as many walls as I have to."

"Good. I'll see you soon."

EMIKO BEGAN her morning hand-to-hand combat classes with Whelkin, which taught her little to nothing. Occasionally she'd pick up an interesting way to disarm or incapacitate someone that she hadn't known, but mostly, she was reviewing basics.

Their private evening sessions, however, took everything she had.

She wondered how the others he trained were faring. Were they doing better than her? Had anyone given up?

Surely the brutal sessions had weeded out one or two hopefuls. Or maybe more. There was no way to know how many people he was working with. She never considered quitting, though. She thought of pain as a road that would take her to her desired destination. If it had to hurt to become a better fighter, she had no complaints. She was no stranger to it.

After a particularly challenging session with Whelkin, Emiko applied dermacare patches to her ribs, sternum, and back, hissing between her teeth as she did so. The patches would take a day to do what a techbed could do in minutes, but she didn't want to run to the infirmary every time she got a booboo. She wasn't a child, and the officials watching her progress might track such things. She could handle some bruised ribs.

She'd stocked up on dermacare and liniment. At every meal, she'd been eating Bennite food, too, which had many health benefits. She wanted to ensure she'd be sufficiently healed for her next lesson.

The way Whelkin taught made sense to her, and her skills

improved with every session. She needed to be in top form, though.

Three months into her life as an academy student, she felt well-adjusted to the routine. She ate to fuel her body, but her classes and her training were the real food she craved. She attended regular meetings of the holo-vid club with Jane. The food appreciation gatherings happened less frequently, due to the effort it took to arrange them, but Emiko and Val had learned a great deal at the two that had taken place so far.

The academy arranged regular social and entertainment events as well, which gave students an opportunity to learn and make new friends. An outdoor concert on the quad with music played by the students of the nearby music college had been announced to a great deal of enthusiasm. It was a yearly event, and apparently one that had a reputation of being great fun.

"How's this?" Jane carried a blanket, while Emiko held a container of tall smoothies they planned to enjoy while listening.

"Perfect," Val said. "We'll have a nice view from here, but won't be so close that ducking out early would get a lot of attention."

"Why would we duck out early?" Emiko asked.

Val shrugged. "No particular reason. I just like to be prepared."

"I like that about you." Emiko said it jokingly, but she meant it. Val had good judgment, which Emiko valued greatly.

They spread their blanket and settled in, sipping their smoothies and talking about their classes. Emiko was glad they'd shown up early. Latecomers ended up crowding around the edges, forced to stand. At least they'd be able to hear well, even if their view wasn't the best. The quad's acoustics were surprisingly good. Some architect of outdoor design had done an excellent job.

The concert opened on a fun note, with a band using electrical instruments to play some recent popular music. From there, the performances showcased just about every musical style Emiko could imagine, and a few she never had and didn't particularly care for.

Overall, she found the performances enjoyable. Sometimes outings like this were tedious or boring, but this one held her attention. Her mind didn't keep skipping ahead to the physics homework waiting for her or any of a dozen other things she could be doing instead.

For a rare couple of hours, she simply enjoyed herself.

Then it was over and they were gathering up the blanket they were sitting on and their trash. As Emiko pushed the cups into the recycler, a good-looking Zerellian guy approached.

"Did you like the music?" he asked.

She checked around, but he was talking to her. Why? "Yes, it was great," she said. "You played cello, right?"

His forehead lifted. "You recognized me?"

Her memory often came in handy. She smiled and nodded.

He tossed a wrapper into the recycler. "Found that on the ground. Some people are so rude."

"Yep. Well, it was nice to meet you. Congratulations on a lovely performance." She almost bowed, but caught herself. She had already gotten into the habit of proper PAC protocol. Being a musician and not a student of the academy, though, he might find it weird.

He reached out as if to touch her arm to keep her from leaving, but pulled his hand back before he made contact. "You wouldn't be free to show me around, would you? I've never been here, and would love to get a good look at the campus."

He smiled and a dimple sank into his right cheek. He was very attractive, and seemed genuine. She bet that dimple got him a lot of dates.

"I'm afraid I have to get to my schoolwork. But let me introduce you to my friends. I'm pretty sure they'd be happy to."

Emiko transferred Mr. Cello into the capable and very interested hands of Jane, then made a hasty retreat.

She was happy to leave flirting with cute musicians and dating to Val and Jane. No doubt it was fun, but Emiko didn't have time to waste on that kind of thing.

As she returned to her dorm and began her bedtime routine, she thought about all the mass of students who had lingered after the concert, socializing, flirting, and no doubt planning to stay up later than they should. They were young, after all, and most were living on their own for the first time in their lives.

Even for Emiko, the switch from having parents noting her schedule, behavior, and what she ate to having complete privacy and control over her life had been a heady thing.

On the other hand, she probably had far less privacy than she liked to think. No doubt she received particular scrutiny every day from people watching to see if she'd live up to her potential, or crack under the pressure.

Regardless, unlike other students, Emiko couldn't afford to be exhausted the next day. She had intensive combat training to do. As much as she loved life at the academy and felt more in her element than she ever had before, she still felt like an outlier. It wasn't a bad thing, exactly. The best of the best, by definition, was an outlier, and that's what she was determined to be.

Sure, she felt isolated sometimes. But it was a price she was willing to pay.

2

Emiko turned her head slightly to avoid the sunlight that kept making her squint. She took a deep breath of fresh air and gave her shoulders a slow roll to loosen the muscles.

Six months into her first year at the academy, she had finally found her groove. She felt like she had all the balls up in the air and was juggling them just as she was supposed to.

She was earning top marks in all of her classes, she continued to progress in her combat skills with Whelkin, and she had established herself as a well-adjusted, normal student.

For the first time in her life, she felt like she was really in the right place and making inroads into the life she had always wanted for herself.

Hand-to-hand combat class was a drain, though. She had to square off against students who had little or no previous training. It felt like babysitting. So far, that morning had been particularly tedious.

Such classes were no fun at all when people were afraid of getting hit. She wondered if these students were merely fulfilling a requirement or if they'd thought this would be an easy class they could make a good grade in without much effort.

Hah.

She renewed her resolve to see these classes as an opportunity to maintain a cover identity. Instead of being a tedious waste of time these sessions provided her with practice at persevering through a tough situation.

She really tried to see it that way. Sitting there with the sun in her eyes watching a couple of softies circle each other was damn boring, though.

At least they were out on the quad that afternoon. Whelkin liked to change up their location each week. She'd seen firsthand how some students lost their fighting nerve outside of the dojo or the boxing ring. She approved of Whelkin's efforts to keep the students from unconsciously thinking that fighting only happened in designated places.

Like Emiko and her classmates, Whelkin himself wore the close-fitting shirt and pants meant for close-contact training. He was a charismatic teacher, and his low-key style usually elicited a hardworking response from his students.

Some people just weren't cut out for fighting, though.

She tried not to cringe as she watched a pair of students skittishly circling one another. Their teacher called out encouragements and corrections, and the two were visibly trying, but they clearly didn't understand the joy of a good fight. They should have dropped out of it weeks ago.

Whelkin's attention caught on something, and he called, "Drew! Join us for a moment, if you have time."

A tall, long-limbed guy about her age trotted over. He had smooth skin, wavy light brown hair he wore just a touch longer than most male academy students, and was very good-looking. As he got closer, she saw that his eyes were brown, but a lighter shade of brown than hers.

Whelkin gestured to her, calling her to the makeshift sparring

ring. She leaped up from her knees in one motion and joined him and the newcomer.

The guy openly studied her. Sized her up. Her interest in this interaction skyrocketed. He wasn't afraid to fight, and he wasn't dismissing her for her size, either, although she stood fifty centimeters shorter and was at least fifty pounds lighter.

Whelkin said, "Drew, this is Emiko. She's my best student in the afternoon class. Emiko, Drew is the best student from my morning class."

Her interest peaked even higher. Was her teacher introducing her to this guy as more than just a demonstration for the other students? Was he good enough to give her a challenge?

They bowed politely to each other in equal measure. She saw in his stance, the set of his shoulders, and the coolness in his eyes that though he didn't discount her as an opponent, he intended to win.

She didn't intend to let him, but she hoped he'd make her work for it.

"I'd like the two of you to show the others how this is done." Whelkin gestured to the rest of the class, who sat watching.

Drew wore the cargo pants and t-shirt typical of academy students rather than the usual sparring clothes. "Sure." He slipped his shoulder out of his backpack strap.

Emiko nodded. *I hope you like losing.*

They stepped into the space, facing each other. Whelkin shouted, "Begin!"

Neither of them moved. Drew gave her time to make the first strike, but she only watched him. He stepped to his right and she moved with him, keeping the space between them constant. She liked that he took time to size up his opponent.

She liked to do that, too.

After circling each other for an unusually long time, he struck. She blocked the light jab, along with the next one. He threw another, faster this time. And again, harder. She easily turned each strike aside and he increased the power behind them until he was hitting his hardest.

Still, she either blocked each blow, or moved out of the way.

Once she felt like she had his measure, she jabbed at his face, then threw a hard punch to his sternum. He dodged the first but the second glanced off his ribs.

She was much stronger than she looked, and now he knew it.

Wisely, he changed tactics, stepping into her space to grapple. It was a smart choice, but he was still too slow. He didn't have the reflexes she'd spent almost all her life developing. From there, it was easy. A knee, a weight shift, and a push put him flat on his ass.

He immediately leaped back to his feet, moving in again to let fly with a solid three-punch combination. Block, block, and she took a solid hit to the chest to get herself in position to put his arm in a vice. His ass was on the ground again.

"Excellent," Whelkin called as Drew leaped to his feet again. "Thank you both."

Drew and Emiko eyed one another, each making sure the other had turned off battle mode before dropping their guard. She felt slightly out of breath from that hit to the chest, but otherwise felt fantastic.

Fighting was the only thing she loved as much as flying. And since flight classes wouldn't begin until her second year, she'd have to get her highs from combat.

"You can't be afraid to take a punch," Whelkin lectured her classmates. "Sometimes you give up a hit to gain the advantage. The more punches you take, the better you'll get at it."

He turned his attention to Drew and Emiko. "Nice work, you two. Emiko, why don't you take off early while I teach your classmates some basics?" He gave her a wink.

She smiled, bowed low to her teacher, and retrieved her backpack. After putting it on, she gave Drew a shallow but proper bow for a fellow student, then turned to leave.

"Hey," he said as she turned away. She looked back at him. "Are you up for an early dinner?" He wore an easy smile.

She immediately began devising the right thanks-but-no-thanks response. She had work to do. She promised her nonexistent roommate they'd eat together. She had an activity scheduled. But then she stopped. Maybe it was his smile, or maybe it was how much more suited to fighting he was compared to her classmates. Something about him made her want to say yes.

So she did.

THE NEXT DAY, Emiko bumped into Drew as she left her first class.

He broke into an easy grin when he saw her. "Hey, I know you. Were you just in there?"

"Nah, I just wander around and pretend to leave classes just as they end. It adds to my mystique."

He laughed. "Fair enough. I'll see you around, then."

After her second class, she crossed the quad toward the cafeteria. Her classes lined up a little oddly, so that her lunchtime always came late. Sometimes she skipped it in lieu of a snack she ate on the run, but her stomach was letting her know that wouldn't be acceptable today.

"Are you stalking me?"

She looked up to see Drew coming from the other direction, looking sweaty but pleased. "I most certainly am not. Are you stalking me?"

"Maybe." From another guy, that response would have put her off, but accompanied by his easy grin, it just seemed funny. And maybe just a touch flirtatious. He seemed to be the kind of guy who made friends and flirted easily, so she didn't take it too seriously, though.

"Have you eaten lunch?" she surprised herself by asking.

"Yeah, but I didn't have time for much. Whelkin's class always makes me extra hungry, too. So if that was an invitation, I accept."

For some reason, she felt her cheeks flush. Was she embarrassed? Pleased? Both? She wasn't used to...well, whatever this was. "It's always nicer to have someone to talk to over a meal, right?"

He made for a good lunch companion. He was a talker, and didn't seem to mind filling in her occasional silences with conversation that was sometimes clever, often intelligent, and frequently funny.

He had an outgoing, laid-back personality that made him easy to get along with and easy to be with. The more time she spent with him, the more he drew her out of her studious shell. She felt less like she had to make an effort to be social and more like she'd found someone she could relax and be her whole self with.

Well, her whole fake self with, anyway.

The thought soured her mood. He seemed entirely genuine and forthcoming, while she was lying about where she came from and even her own name. Maybe it was wrong of her to make friends with him under that pretense.

It hadn't stopped her from making friends with Val and Jane, though. So why would he be different?

She felt uneasy when they parted ways after eating. She should probably make an effort not to cross paths with him tomorrow after her first class and before lunch. If they kept spending time together, she'd just have to keep feeling this way.

Better to just avoid it. She didn't have time for distractions.

Whelkin's class in the afternoon turned out to be fun because not only did they go out to the quad again, but he also used her to demonstrate some advanced concepts. They didn't go over anything that he'd been teaching her in their private lessons, but it was much higher-level stuff than she usually got to do in class.

When they were done, she noticed that Drew had taken a seat near the class.

So much for making sure they didn't cross paths. Never had she failed so quickly at a new resolution.

"Now I'm starting to think you really are stalking me," she said to him as they shrugged on their backpacks. She smiled to make sure he knew she was kidding.

"You wish. This place is crawling with girls who want me to stalk them. You and I just happen to have schedules that coincide. What do you have left today?"

She should make some excuse to leave without telling him, or just lie to create some distance. For some reason, though, she actually detailed the rest of her day.

Then he detailed his afternoon and evening, and his next day, too.

Though his major was systems engineering, they had a lot of the same core classes. No wonder they kept crossing paths.

But wouldn't it be nice to be able to compare notes with someone, or complain about a teacher to someone who could understand? Val and Jane took entirely different classes, and Emiko rarely saw them during the daytime unless they ran into each other at the dorm.

She could be friends with him. She'd just have to be careful.

WITHIN A WEEK, Emiko's schedule had dovetailed with Drew's. They walked together when they were headed the same direction and began eating lunch together every day. Everyone seemed to know him, and he attracted a variety of different people who joined them.

She'd started to get used to eating a quick lunch alone while studying, but eating as a group turned out to be kind of nice. It gave her a chance to meet more people, too.

When the weekend arrived, she was glad. As much as she liked seeing Drew, they'd jumped right into spending a lot of time together, and a little distance would be good. She spent the first day studying and didn't even leave for food. Instead, she ordered some delivery and spooned Bennite stew into her mouth as she worked on her physics homework.

Her voicecom alerted her to an incoming message. She opened a channel.

"Hey, stalker." Drew grinned at her.

She blinked at him. "You called me."

"Yeah. I've been in my room all day and need sunlight, or I'll wilt like a fern."

"Most Earth ferns don't like direct sunlight," she said.

"Really? Man. You should have told me that before. But why are you a fern expert?"

She laughed. "I'm not. I just read it somewhere once."

"Huh. Okay. But anyway, do you want to meet me on the quad?"

"Why?"

"Sunlight. Fresh air. Recreation."

When she didn't immediately answer, he added, "I'll bring you some ice cream."

She rolled her shoulders. She *was* getting a little stiff from sitting all day. "All right. Make sure it's chocolate, though, or the deal is off."

"Duly noted."

She double-checked to make sure she'd saved her physics work, then turned off the voicecom display. She should check to see if Val and Jane were available. They'd like Drew, and hanging out as a group would make sure things remained casual between them. She could send him a message on her comport to tell him to bring them ice cream, too.

They didn't answer their door, though, which left her on her own.

"Look," he said suddenly.

Emiko had thoroughly enjoyed her ice cream, which had been a rather large portion. After eating their frozen treats, they'd stretched out on the blanket he'd spread and watched their classmates playing a friendly game of discball. She followed his gaze, looking up toward the sky, but saw nothing noteworthy. No planes or drones or skydivers. "At what?"

"That cloud." He pointed. "What does it look like to you?"

She'd been lying on her right side, propping her head up on her hand, so she rolled onto her back. "Just clouds."

"No, you're not looking right." He turned around and lay down on his back beside her. He pointed up, so she could follow the precise direction of his finger. "Right there. That one. What does it look like?"

It looked like a cloud, but he'd be disappointed if she didn't come up with a more whimsical answer. She squinted at it, which didn't help. Then she let her focus drift slightly to the right of the cloud in question.

"Wait, a duck, right? With some sort of hat."

"Yes! A very pointy hat." He slapped her a high five. "Anything else?"

She sighed and went back to looking at clouds. This was childish and entirely unproductive. But it was fun.

"That one." She stabbed her finger toward the sky. "It's an interstellar ship."

"Really? How can you tell it's interstellar, and not just some atmospheric ship?"

"Just a feeling."

He rolled over to look at her. "Maybe you just like atmospheric ships better?"

She smiled. "Maybe."

He gave her a long look, and she was ready to roll away and

jump into some ass-kicking. But he didn't move toward her. "Let me guess. You're a pilot."

Should she admit to it? He already knew she was studying security, and there didn't seem to be a reason not to tell her that she studied avionics, too. "Yes. But what made you think so?"

"You have that adrenaline-junkie vibe."

"I do not." She sat up, not sure what to think of his pronouncement.

"Sure you do. The way you like to fight? And it's that you like it, not just that you're good at it. Then there's your whole way-too-serious thing."

She laughed. "I'm not too serious. I'm just serious enough. And you know, I object to your saying that I'm a type. I'm a unique individual."

He grinned. "I figured that out. But guess what? So am I."

"A unique individual or an adrenaline junkie?"

"Well, I meant the first thing, but maybe a little of the second, too. Not like you, though. I can tell you're a straight-up psycho." He rolled his eyes and stuck out his tongue.

Laughing, she gave his shoulder a playful shove.

"Seriously, though," he said. "Think you could spar with me sometime? Teach me some things?"

"I've never taught anyone. Shouldn't you work with Whelkin?"

"I am. I will. But is there such a thing as studying too much?" He had that look in his eye, the one he'd had when she first met him. The one that had made her notice him as different from others.

Different in the same way that she was different.

"We could try."

"WHAT ABOUT YORK HALL?" Drew suggested.

"I checked it out yesterday. Too much traffic."

"Whitman?"

"Maybe. Let's go see." Without giving him any warning, she took off running.

They'd already looked around three buildings for a room that didn't get any use. Of course, that meant that the ones with classrooms and administrative offices were out of the question. People would notice them coming and going on a regular basis and might start to wonder why.

Residence halls had seemed more likely, so they'd begun touring the basements of the ones that had enough traffic that Drew and Emiko wouldn't look conspicious going in and out. Someplace that might have unused storage space or service areas that were no longer utilized.

Though she heard his feet pounding the ground behind her, she made it to Whitman Hall first. With a "Hah!" of triumph, she opened the door for him.

"I like how courteous you are, even when you're gloating." He booped her nose as he entered. "Let's find the lift."

"This way." She'd committed the blueprints of the residence halls to memory, which made their search a little easier. Of course, what the blueprints didn't show was how the building was actually being used.

They stepped into the lift and rode it down into the basement.

"I hope there aren't any spiders." Drew scrunched up his face in faux terror.

"It's a basement. You can bet there will be."

"Nooooo," he moaned. "All those legs freak me out."

"Shhh." She poked him, laughing as the doors opened.

She peeked out, looking for maintenance people.

Nobody. That was a good sign.

Most maintenance and janitorial people worked during the day, which made their nighttime search less risky. Even so, she didn't want to get in trouble for being somewhere they weren't supposed to be.

She didn't want that kind of thing on her record.

"I like how quiet it is down here," he murmured.

"Yeah. All we need is a decent-sized room. Assuming it's like this most of the time, this could work."

"Well, we shouldn't assume," he pointed out. "You know what happens."

She sighed and tried to look aggrieved, but he grinned. He knew she didn't mean it.

The first room held the building's self-contained air-filtration unit. According to PAC regulations, each building had to have one. They moved down the hall and found janitorial storage.

"Let's try this way." He made a left turn down a hall.

"I'm not seeing any doors." She skimmed a hand along the wall, imagining their location on the blueprint. They'd just gone past the exterior wall of the first floor. They were probably somewhere under the sidewalk that led out the back side of the building.

"There's got to be one somewhere. I'm sure they didn't build this hallway just as a dead-end practical joke." His voice bounced off the enclosed space.

"Wait, there it is." Ahead, the hallway curved slightly, then ended with a door. "This is kind of ominous. I bet there's a werewolf in there."

"Vampires," he declared. "Definitely vampires. This is where they bring people to drain them of their blood. It's far enough away from anything else that no one hears the screams."

"Planning ahead is key," she said agreeably.

She loved that he shared her dark sense of humor.

The room probably stored some kind of volatile chemicals that required a minimum distance from living quarters. It would probably also be locked.

She was surprised when the door opened.

The room was huge. Nearly the size of one of the cafeterias on campus, and practically empty. It was perfect.

"It's filthy." Drew's lip curled in disgust. "And the smell..."

"Nothing a little cleaning won't fix." She walked slowly around the space, trying to figure out why it was there.

"A little? It would take days. Several very dirty days."

"Afraid of a little dirty work?" She arched a mocking eyebrow at him before squatting down to examine deep divots in the floor along the southern wall. "Oh. This was a laundry. They've removed all the machines, but this is where they'd have hooked into the air-filtration system. Huh."

"Really?" Drew squatted beside her. "A whole room for doing laundry?"

"Yeah. Back before they had compact processors. Since we all have one in our room, places like this became obsolete."

"And since this place is inconveniently located, it doesn't get used," he surmised.

"Exactly." She grinned at him. "It's perfect."

"It is."

She suddenly became aware of his nearness. His face was only half a meter away, and his left knee bumped against her right.

Something between them shifted, and the size of the universe shrank down to the small space they occupied. Time seemed to slow.

He scooted closer and put his arm around her back. She put her hand on his knee to steady them both, and they met in the middle for a long, but gentle kiss. It ought to have been awkward and ridiculous, but it wasn't.

He pulled back slightly and grinned. "So...I guess we're going to have to get some cleaning supplies."

She laughed, a little out of breath. "I guess so."

"Let's start tomorrow." He stood and pulled her up.

She liked that he hadn't made a big deal about the kiss. No

cheesy compliments about her eyes or that he really liked her. It had simply happened, and now they were focused on the subject at hand.

Her excitement about the possibilities of their newfound treasure bubbled up. She was in a great mood, in spite of the dirty work ahead of them. "I'll bring the cleansers. You bring the scrub brushes."

AFTER THREE DAYS of intensive cleaning efforts, Emiko and Drew had themselves a private little dojo. They brought in some mats and chairs and a small folding table.

It was perfect. They immediately began training together.

Drew improved each time they sparred. She rarely had to correct him twice. His rapid advancement impressed her. She'd trained with a lot of people over the years, but she'd never seen someone improve so rapidly.

They'd taken to running together each morning before classes, and most days they met up between classes, too. She'd only known him for a month, but they saw progressively more and more of each other.

He still had trouble hitting her when they sparred. Not getting hit was kind of her specialty. She ducked under punches, leaned back, turned aside, and generally just made sure she wasn't in the way of wherever he was hitting. Unless she wanted to use his force against him, of course.

She found an opening between his attacks. Trapping his arm as it was extended and all of his force was aligned behind it, she stopped him in place. With both of her hands trapping his arm, she leaned forward, extended her right leg up, all the way above and over her head, and lightly tapped him on the head with it.

The lightning-fast motion took only a moment, and she stepped back afterward.

The look on his face was priceless. It was a mixture of surprise and awe.

"How did you do that?" he asked.

She laughed. He had a way of making her laugh that no one else ever had. "It's not something you'd ever use in real combat. I can do it a lot harder than that, but it's really just a showy thing I created for extra points in competition. Judges loved it when competitors scored a touch in a creative way."

"Well, it's cool. What else did you do for creativity points?"

She smiled, remembering her competition days. Unexpected moves had been her specialty. "I did a lot of flips. Things you would almost never do in a real fight."

"Show me."

"Really?" She looked at him to see if he was teasing her. He liked to tease.

"Really." This time, he was earnest.

She looked around, concerned about someone seeing, but the basement was deserted, as always. In the three weeks they'd been doing this, no one had ever taken notice of them entering Whitman Hall, and they'd never encountered anyone else in the basement.

"Okay," she agreed.

She executed a forward tucked flip, a backward layout flip, and—her favorite—a tucked sideways flip that covered a lot of ground.

"Wow." Drew seemed impressed. "Think you could teach me?"

She eyed him and wrinkled her nose. "I'm not sure. It's a lot tougher for taller people. Maybe you could do a back tuck?"

"Show me."

The rest of that session became more about gymnastics than combat. He fell on the mat over and over, even with her spotting him. She liked that he never got frustrated or angry, no matter how many times he fell. He either laughed, grimaced, or both, and got back up.

"I think that's enough for today," she said after he took a particularly hard fall. "This isn't something you get right in one session, or even a week."

"Sure." He pulled himself up into a sitting position, squinting a little.

"I have a major stockpile of dermacare," she said.

He grinned up at her. "Are you inviting me to your room?"

"Uh..." She hadn't thought that far ahead. So far, all of their interactions had been in public spaces. Letting him come to her room felt like it would be more personal, somehow.

Considering their kiss earlier, which had proved that they definitely weren't just friends, she hesitated to push things further.

"I'm kidding." He stood and dusted himself off. "I didn't mean to make you nervous."

"Who said I was nervous?" she fired back. "It's just dermacare. Let's go."

TWENTY MINUTES LATER, she doubted her decision. She didn't mind that he was in her room, but his shirt was off and her fingers were on his skin as she helped him get the dermacare patches into place.

What was wrong with her? She'd done this tons of times for other people. With Drew, though, she felt alive in a way she'd never felt before, except for when she was fighting or piloting a ship. All of her nerve endings were on alert, and she felt hyper-aware of every detail around her.

She snatched her hand back when she felt like she'd been smoothing the edges of the patch for too long.

"Thanks." He grinned as he pulled his shirt over his head.

She should have felt relieved, but the shirt made little difference. He was still there, filling the small space of her room with his smile and the smooth sound of his voice and the way he had of moving that was just so much more appealing than the way any other person moved.

What was it about him? How could she like him so much after knowing him only a month?

"Should we do you now?" he asked, picking up another patch.

"I'm good," she said quickly. "Already have one on."

"Why?" he asked. "That class you have with Whelkin can't possibly give you any challenge."

She couldn't exactly tell him about her much more intensive private lessons with Whelkin. "You know," she said thoughtfully, "I think you'll be able to do that flip within a couple of weeks."

"I'll keep working at it." He stepped closer. "But you didn't answer my question."

"I was hoping to distract you," she admitted.

"I figured that out already." He moved even closer. "Why?"

When she hesitated, he said, "Be honest. Always be honest with me. Even if there's something you can't tell me, just say you can't tell me."

"Will that be enough?" She couldn't decide if she should move closer to him or edge away.

"Yes. Whatever you can share is enough. Just don't lie to me. Sound fair?"

"Okay." The electricity between them was enlivening every cell in her body, but she didn't want him to misunderstand her. "The truth is, my career in the PAC is everything to me. Anything else is secondary. No, not even that. Nothing will get in the way of my career. I like you, but I'm not...girlfriend material. I don't have time for that stuff. I have to work."

He caught her wrist and ran his fingers down her hand to twine with hers. "That's why we fit. I'm not boyfriend material, because I'm determined to finish at the top of my class and make it into OTS. I'm not looking to waste time on holding hands and watching holo-vids, or doing each other's hair, or whatever dating people do."

She snickered. "I don't think they do that."

She didn't pull her hand away. In fact, the gap between them was closing, and she wasn't sure which one of them was causing it.

"I wouldn't know." He put his other arm around her, at her waist.

"Me either." She leaned into him. "I've never been interested in anything more than casual dates."

"Neither have I. I'm way too busy for that stuff."

"Me too." She put her hands on his waist.

"Good," he said, leaning down to her.

"Good," she agreed, rising up to him.

He kissed her, and she kissed him, and they were definitely not a couple, but that didn't matter, because they were completely the same.

IT DIDN'T TAKE Val and Jane long to notice Drew. They saw him in the hall of their dorm, and caught a glimpse of Emiko with him on campus. Three months after meeting him, he'd become a constant in her life. They studied together, ate together, and trained together. Somehow they never quite got a proper introduction, though, thanks to differing schedules and odd luck.

"He's gorgeous!" Val enthused one afternoon when Emiko had gone over to help her neighbors rearrange their furniture. It was a peculiar thing they did every few weeks, made odder by the fact that even in their larger, double room, there wasn't much space.

"You should bring him to the holo-vid club. Where did you meet him?" Jane asked.

Emiko sat on the edge of the desk she'd just moved. "We just ran into each other on campus one day. We had a lot in common. You know."

She hoped they knew. Both of them had dated, as normal people did. She was only pretending she knew about romance.

But they nodded knowingly, so she must have guessed accurately.

"Is it serious?" Val asked, sitting on her bed.

"No. I don't have time for a serious relationship, and neither does he."

Jane got a sly look. "So it's purely physical? Nice."

"No!" As soon as she said it, she knew she should have simply agreed. It would make a simpler story. But she couldn't define Drew as some plaything. They weren't a couple, per se, but they weren't nothing, either. "We just have a lot in common, and work well together."

"I bet you do," Jane said with a leer. Val slapped her a high five.

"Nothing like that. I mean study-wise. We're taking a lot of the same subjects, though our classes are at different times."

Jane laughed. "We're just kidding. And kind of jealous."

Val tugged at her bed. "Help me with this, will you?"

Emiko moved next to her. "Where's it going?"

"Along that wall." Jane pointed.

Emiko got a grip on the headboard and pushed it from the wall. A hot knife of pain lit up the right side of her ribcage.

Both of her friends immediately fell upon her. "What happened? Did you hurt your back? Are your arms or legs numb?"

She tried to brush them off. "No, no, I'm fine. Just a little sore from training."

But they wouldn't be deterred. Jane pulled up her shirt and hissed at the spreading black and purple bruises she saw beneath.

"What's this?" Jane demanded as she pulled away the dermacare patch to see the entirety.

"Just training. Like I said. It's nothing."

"It's not nothing," Val argued. "You've had severe bruising, and what looks like a hematoma or two. Why haven't you been to the infirmary?"

"Handling things is part of the job I'm training for. I want them to see that I'm not going to run for help for minor issues. None of this is a serious injury. They go away in a few days."

Val and Jane exchanged a dark look.

"Okay. You don't want to go to the infirmary. That's fine. But why didn't you come to us?" Jane looked hurt. "We could fix this up for you easy."

"You could?"

Val retrieved a medkit from her backpack. "Yeah, dummy. That's what *we're* training for. So how about you do what you do, and you let us do what we do? Deal?"

Emiko hesitated.

"What, you don't trust us?" Jane taunted. "You think we'll cut off your arm or something while healing some bruises?"

"No, I just..." How could she explain to them that she wanted to prove that she was tough enough for the job she wanted?

"Think of it as helping us out with some practice," Jane suggested, holding Emiko's shirt out of the way so Val could run a medical device over her injuries.

"And it's not like we can tell anyone. Patient confidentiality, you know," Val added.

Emiko smiled. "Okay, then. When you put it that way."

They set to work, and in just a few minutes, had healed all of her bruises and sore spots.

"I could have fixed this for you last night after the dinner club. Instead, you've been walking around with all this. Just let us know when you get new ones. It's bad to get new bruises on top of old ones." Val waved the device at her in warning.

"I will."

"Good." Jane looked satisfied. "Now help me move this bed."

That evening, Emiko added an unscheduled social occasion to her daily activities. She, Jane, and Val met up with Drew and a friend of his on the quad, then had dinner together.

An officer must be flexible, after all.

BY THE END of Emiko's first year at the academy, she'd found her stride. She battled for top marks in all of her classes, trained hard with Whelkin, and trained still more with Drew. They ran, sparred, and lifted weights together. She hung out with Val and Jane on a regular basis, and they made sure she stayed in peak physical condition.

She'd never been so happy, fighting with all her might to make strides toward the future she wanted.

When the break between year one and year two came, she didn't want to go home. She couldn't wait to see her parents and brother because it had been three months since she'd visited, but she didn't want to live at home again. It would feel like going backward when she only wanted to keep forging ahead.

She'd avoided that for the summer break by enrolling for supplemental sprint courses. Drew had done the same, while Val and Jane had gone to Jane's hometown to enjoy some downtime.

No classes were offered during the end-of-year break, though. Plus, her parents were eager to spend some time with her. There was nothing to do but go home.

Seeing Val and Jane off was simple. She'd see them in eight weeks. It was different with Drew.

They ran together in the morning, as usual, but didn't spar or study. They had breakfast, took a walk, and sat on the quad and people-watched. It was the closest thing to a real date they'd ever had, other than the day they'd eaten ice cream and looked at clouds on the quad.

She didn't want to say goodbye to him, even for eight weeks. After nearly a year of sharing their lives, the thought of being without him left her feeling bereft. He'd become her partner in the fight to become officers.

He tickled her earlobe. "Cheer up. We'll be back to work before you know it."

"I know. It'll be fine."

They sat on their favorite bench, under a tall tree. She didn't know what kind of tree, since she had no particular interest in horticulture. It was pretty, though, with a thick trunk and wide branches that gave them just the right amount of shade.

"It will. And when we start back, we'll be second years and you'll get to start flight training."

She smiled. He always knew the right thing to say.

He didn't ask where she was going, and she didn't ask him, either. More and more, over the months they'd been together, she'd begun to believe that he, too, planned on clandestine ops. He was as driven as she was, and threw himself into physical training like no one else she knew.

Well, like only she did.

They managed to be fiercely competitive with each other, always vying for the top mark in the classes they had in common, but always glad for the other when they got it. It was the kind of competition that made them better rather than dividing them.

Everything about being with him made her life better. Which was why she wasn't looking forward to the weeks ahead.

"And you've gone dark again." He tickled her ear again, but she couldn't muster a smile.

"Sorry."

"Don't be sorry." He put his arm around her. "I'm glad you're pining for me before we've even left. It's good for my ego. Makes me feel manly."

She laughed. He had such a weird, ego-free sense of humor that his claiming to have an ego was funny in itself.

He affected a hurt expression. "I say I'm manly and she laughs. I may need to ponder on this. It may lead to some insecurity issues. Possibly a minor complex or two."

She leaned her head against him. "It'll be good to get back to work, once we return."

"Yup."

They spent their remaining time that way, talking about nothing in particular and trying to hang onto the moment.

3

Emiko's trip home felt like entering an alternate timeline. As soon as she stepped into her parents' home, it was like the events of the past year went into purgatory while she resumed the life she'd led before.

Her mother fussed over her with food and tea and making sure she wasn't cold, while her father tried to ask questions about school that were as broad and unassuming as he could make them.

He knew she was after clandestine ops, and she knew he knew, but they both pretended neither of them knew. He knew the game better than she did, having worked in central intelligence for the past couple of decades. It didn't introduce any weirdness between them because at home, she was just her parents' daughter and her brother's sister.

Those were good things to be, and she liked being with her family. She loved them dearly, and they were unreserved in their affection for her. But after a week, she grew restless. Each day, she trained longer and longer. She focused on weapons training, which she hadn't done much of thus far at the academy.

At the end of the second week, her father entered their little home dojo as she was finishing up a training session. She was sweating and tired, and felt like she'd accomplished something.

"You're ready to go back to school, aren't you?" he asked without preamble.

"What? No, I—" She stopped. She could tell he knew the truth. "It's not that I don't want to be home. I love you guys."

A strand of hair had escaped her ponytail, and he tucked it behind her ear, just as he'd done all her life. It made her feel like she was six years old, but in a good way. "I know. But you're on the path now, and focused on your goal. You'll be restless until you meet your goal. I get it. I was once just like you."

She looked at her father, a middle-aged Japanese man with a chin just like hers. They were so much alike. Of course he understood. "What about Mom?"

"She'll be upset for you to leave so soon, but don't worry. I'll remind her of what I was like at your age. She'll understand. She's a career-minded woman, herself."

At least her brother had already returned to his own school, and she didn't have to worry about disappointing him.

"Are you sure it's okay?" she asked. She felt caught between two worlds, both of which were important to her, but one of them felt more urgent.

"Of course. We both know you have your sights on a big goal, and you have to give it your all."

She hugged him, inhaling the smell that was unique to him. She couldn't even identify it. It was part yuzu and part synthetic leather, but mostly just unique to her dad.

"I won't let you down," she promised him. "I'll be the best. I promise, it will all be worth it."

He cupped the back of her head in his palm. "You have never, and could never, let me down."

She went to her room to pack, and left the handling of her

mother to him. She only needed ten minutes to get her things ready to go, but she remained in her room for another twenty to make sure the situation was smoothed over.

She didn't consider it cowardly. She considered it outsourcing the job to the right person.

Meanwhile, she checked her messages. She and Drew hadn't promised to stay in touch via the voicecom, like all the other couples who separated for the break. To her, it emphasized how different they were from other students, while emphasizing how much they had in common.

She was certain now that he was just like her. He was hiding his first life, just as she was hiding her own. He had to be aiming for clandestine ops, too. It would explain so much.

Throughout the vacation, they never spoke to each other in real time. Instead, they sent each other short text messages daily. Nothing of substance. Just a sentence or two, usually a funny observation or anecdote. It was enough to say all the things they couldn't say.

Finally, when she felt she'd given her dad enough time to prepare her mom, she pulled her PAC Academy hoodie over her head and left the safety of her bedroom.

"Everything okay out here?" she ventured.

Her parents were in the kitchen making tea.

"Of course," her mother said. "You two act like I don't know what it's like to be driven. I do work in the diplomatic corps, you know. I may be your mother, but I also know a thing or two about ambition."

Emiko felt relief wash over her. "Thanks, Mom."

Her mother made a shooing gesture. "None of that. Let's have tea, then we'll get you to the transport station. We'll be right on time for you to catch a tram."

Returning to campus was a relief, but also strange. She got off the tram and walked the rest of the way to campus. As she got closer, the familiar bustle of life failed to greet her. Although normally a place of constant activity, the academy was nearly deserted. Emiko saw a groundskeeper trimming some shrubs, but otherwise, she noticed no one else. Once she got to the quad, she saw a pair of students throwing a flying disk back and forth. One of them waved, and she waved back, but since she didn't know them, she kept on.

Arriving at her dorm felt like a homecoming. More so, oddly, than returning to her parents' house. Being there had felt like going back in time. Only now did she feel like she had returned to her current life. Like she'd gotten herself back on track.

She was alone, but no matter. She'd get a jump-start on the next year's work. And she'd weight train at the gym. She had all the academy's resources at her disposal, and she'd use them well.

She sent a message to Drew. *Returned to campus early, so get ready for me to beat you at Year Two.*

Smiling, she unpacked her suitcase, putting her things neatly into drawers and stowing the suitcase in her closet. It reminded of her of when she'd first arrived at the academy almost a year ago. She felt like she'd gained about ten years of experience in that short amount of time.

She pulled her hoodie off and hung it in the closet. Smoothing her hair, she decided she'd do some math study.

Before she could sit down in the comfy chair she'd bought when she'd first moved in, her door chime sounded. Someone she knew must have seen her walking across campus. They were probably glad to have someone to talk to. She wouldn't mind, either, truth be told.

Maybe Drew was rubbing off on her

She answered the door, but it wasn't just some random student standing there, grinning at her.

"Drew!" She launched herself at him.

He caught her and spun her around. "You recognized me! I thought maybe you'd forgotten what I look like."

"Almost," she said as he set her on her feet. "Another week and you might have escaped my memory entirely."

"That would be a shame. I'd have to win you over with my irresistible charm and wit all over again."

She laughed and tugged him by the hand into her room, feeling excited and happy. "When did you get back?"

"Yesterday."

"And you didn't tell me?" They sat on the bed and snuggled up together.

"I didn't want you to think I was trying to guilt you into coming back."

"Hm." She brushed his hair back from his face. "Do you think I was doing that to you?"

"Nope. If you were manipulative like that, I wouldn't like you so much."

"Is that right?" She found that admission interesting. They rarely said anything about how they felt about each other. They just let their actions speak for them.

"I like that we're completely honest with each other and don't worry about categorizing our relationship. I like that it isn't about ownership or expectations."

She leaned into him. "That's exactly how I feel, too."

"Good. So how are we going to spend the next six weeks?"

"What do you suggest?"

His hand slid behind her neck to tickle the skin at her nape. "I can think of a thing or two."

"Besides that." She laughed.

"I'd like to work on some database administration at the lab. I checked, and it's open, and since no one else will be using it, I can work up some big configurations and do some testing."

"Okay."

"And I want to work on landing that backflip cleanly. I still don't have it just right. And maybe that kick-me-in-the-head-over-your-head thing."

She nodded. "Okay. We can do that."

"And I happen to know that Whelkin's around. What do you say to hitting him up for some training, with both of us?"

"I like it. He did say that I was his best afternoon class student and you were his best morning student." She didn't mention how much she'd taught Drew since the day they'd first met. The truth was, he'd helped her improve, too.

Neither of them said anything about having private lessons with Whelkin, either. She was sure now that he'd had them, though. She'd recognized techniques Whelkin had shown her when Drew had tried them. She was sure he'd noticed the same about her.

It was an unacknowledged secret between them. They were alike in more ways than they could talk about. Rather than being a chasm between them, it was a bond.

She wondered if she'd spend the rest of her life this way, keeping secrets from the people closest to her.

She imagined she would. But then, if the people close to her were like her, that would be okay, wouldn't it?

"Is the cafeteria open?" she asked. She hadn't thought to check.

"Why, are you hungry?"

"I am."

"Well it isn't. But we can get delivery, or we could call a taxi." He patted his stomach. "I could use a meal."

"Let's order in," she decided.

"An excellent choice, Miss. Shall we go with Italian, Zerellian, or Bennite?"

She didn't have to think. "Bennite! Stew and bread. Lots of both."

"Sounds perfect."

"You order it while I visit the necessary. But get it delivered to your room." She disentangled herself from him and stood.

"Why my room?"

"We've eaten here the last few times. We're getting into a rut."

He gasped. "Oh dear, we can't have that! Well, Miss, go visit the necessary. Take care of nature, wash your hands, and I will order us a monster delivery of stew and bread. Then we shall feast at my abode. It will be glorious. A tale for the ages."

She laughed on her way down the hall. He was so silly sometimes.

She loved that about him.

IF WHELKIN WAS SURPRISED to see her on his doorstep with Drew beside her, he didn't show it. Maybe he'd introduced them for a reason. Maybe he already knew how they'd hit it off, and how much time they spent together.

Emiko suspected that the people who mattered paid close attention to everything she did. Regardless of what he did or didn't know, there was something she wanted.

She intended to get it, too.

"You two want to train together?" Whelkin asked before she had the chance to, looking from her to Drew.

"Yes." She returned his gaze, keeping her expression blank, shielding her thoughts. If Whelkin didn't reveal his motives and observations, she wouldn't, either.

"Good. We can start on some two-on-one training. Let's get started."

Whelkin said nothing about them being on campus during break, or why he happened to be available to work with them. He just led them to a training room and got to work.

Three hours later, she was tired and sore, but pleased with the new skills she'd learned.

"Same time tomorrow," Whelkin said before turning to leave. "Get to the infirmary and get yourselves ready for it, because we'll go even harder." He paused at the door, glancing back at them. "The time for managing it on your own with dermacare is over. I expect you to be in peak shape every time we meet."

"Wait!" she called before he could disappear. "Is it a good thing or a bad thing that we handled our aches on our own?"

Whelkin's hard demeanor softened just enough to show a glint of humor. "Well, you haven't been disqualified for anything yet, so take it as you will."

With that he was gone, leaving her and Drew staring after him, pondering his meaning.

"I'm going to take that as deeply, deeply subtle encouragement," Drew decided.

"That's how I interpreted it, too. Yes!" She gave him a high five.

He grinned at her as they gathered up their backpacks. "It doesn't take much to make you happy, does it?"

"Not really. Give me a long stick and a lot of people to hit with it, and that's all I need." She widened her eyes at him, going for a wild, maniacal expression.

"I'm glad we're on the same side," he joked. "Let's hit the infirmary."

Drew improved his combat skills at an impressive pace. Two weeks into their intensive daily practices with Whelkin, she could see his personal style taking shape.

No matter what type of fighting a person did, once they reached a certain level of competence, they developed their own particular style. Tactics and movements they liked best along with what they found most effective for their strength and size combined into a unique set of base tactics.

He was already doing things that had taken her years to learn. She should probably be concerned. He was her competition. They were both gunning for something elite, rare, and offered to a very select few. It might even come down to a her-or-him decision.

Even so, she was nothing but proud of him, and wanted to keep pushing him to get better.

He made her better, too. Hopefully, there would be room for both of them in covert ops.

"Think you could teach me some bo staff?" he asked her one day when they'd already worked with Whelkin and gotten patched up in the infirmary.

"Yeah. We could do that." He was good enough to begin weapons training, and a bo was a good one to start with. "We'll need plenty of space, though. Our basement dojo has too low a ceiling."

"The quad?" he suggested. "Or the gym would work. Since campus is deserted, no one's likely to see us in either place."

He wouldn't have said that if he weren't training for covert ops.

"The quad," she decided. "No walls. Plus, being outside would be nice. It's a pretty day. If anyone does come along, we can quit or leave."

They dropped by her room to pick up the staff, then went to the quad. They brought some lunch with them, for afterward.

Once they got into place, Drew sat down. "Show me some fancy moves. You know, the showy stuff. Inspire me."

She smiled. He had a way of mixing sincerity and humor that was irresistible.

She let out a slow breath, bending her knees slightly. She began her warm-up routine, which involved sweeping arcs and quick jabs to loosen up her shoulder muscles and get her blood flowing. Then she moved faster, reversing the length of the staff and incorporating level changes, crouching low, then standing tall.

Once she felt warmed up, she launched into a routine she'd once done in competition. It involved a lot of reversals of the bo, using one end and then the other, and several spins and throws. Near the end, she planted one end on the ground and used it to launch herself up into a flying kick.

When she was done, she was breathing hard and feeling good.

"Wow. Looks like I have a lot to learn," Drew said.

"Yeah. That routine won me a championship medal."

"I bet. What's it like to do something like that?"

She put the staff down and sat beside it. "What, winning or the form work?"

"I've won a thing or two, myself," he drawled, making her wonder what he was referring to. "I mean doing a routine like that."

"It feels amazing." She searched for the words to describe it. "Doing something that is extremely difficult, but doesn't feel that way because I've practiced it so much. It's like transcending to a whole new level. Your body feels right because it remembers how to do it, and you don't even have to think about it. It's not about thinking, it's just feeling and executing. It's hard to describe."

He nodded slowly. "Let's get started, then."

Over the next hour, she showed him the basics. He had no natural aptitude. He held the bo like it was a bazooka rather than a part of his body. But he worked tirelessly, and never let himself get discouraged.

He was still giving it his all when she said, "That's enough for today."

Another thing she liked about him: he put the staff down, even though she knew he'd like to keep working. She remembered herself, years ago, working hour after hour, working herself into exhaustion. She had been more stubborn. He was just as hardworking, but more willing to listen to expert advice.

It was probably one reason he advanced so quickly. He worked hard, but he also worked smart. He used everything that was available to him, including the expertise of those around him.

She hadn't been nearly so wise in her younger years. She'd always charged ahead and done things her own way. If a square peg hadn't fit into a round hole, she had *made* it fit, by any means necessary.

She was older now, and maybe it was time to change. Time to work smarter. She had a lot she wanted to achieve, and couldn't brute-force her way through all of it.

Only some of it.

"Ready to eat? I'm starved," Drew said, already laying out sandwiches and drinks.

"You're always starved."

"Shut up. So are you." His grin belied his harsh words.

They ate lunch. Afterward they stretched their challenged muscles, lying on their backs, to study the clouds.

It was weird how he liked to do that, but kind of fun, too. She liked his whimsy.

"Look." She pointed urgently. "A porcupine."

"I was thinking evergreen tree, but yeah, I can see a porcupine there, too."

They lapsed into a long silence, soaking up the warm rays of the sun, resting, and just enjoying this time together. Their second year at the academy would be more intense than the first, and they might not see each other as much.

He finally spoke. "So what happens if you don't reach the highest heights? What then?"

"If I make it into OTS, I'll become the best kind of whatever officer I qualify to be."

"And if you don't make it to OTS?"

She had no fall-back. "That's not an option."

"Imagine it, though," he said. "What would you do?"

"No. This is it for me. It's always been. There can be nothing else."

He fell silent for a long time. Finally, he said, "Okay, hard-ass. OTS or bust, then."

He reached for her hand.

"Yeah," she said. "Thanks, though."

"For what?"

"For being here. You've actually managed to make some of this fun."

He squeezed her hand. "It should be fun. The harder things get, the harder we have to work to find the fun. Otherwise, we'll get crushed by all the heavy things coming our way."

"And then what?"

He turned his head to squint at her. "I was thinking that was kind of the end, the being crushed and all. But I guess if something happens after that, it's us trying to dig ourselves out. Because that's how life is."

"Even if we're all mangled and my face is crushed and looks like a bloody fist with a pair of eyeballs in it?"

He gave her shoulder a shove. "Thanks for the visual. But yeah. Even then. We keep going as long as we can."

"Yeah. That sounds right."

"Sooo..." he said, stretching the word out. "We should probably enjoy life while we can. Before your face gets smashed in and all."

She had a good idea where his thoughts were going. "What did you have in mind?"

"I'm glad you asked!" He scooped her over his shoulder and took off at a loping gallop back toward his dorm.

"My bo! Wait, my bo!" She made grabbing motions in its

direction. She didn't care about the picnic basket or blanket, but she'd be damned if she'd leave her weapon behind.

"Right. Sorry." He didn't put her down, though. He went back, grabbed the staff, and resumed course. "We'll come back for the rest."

It was hard to laugh with her stomach pressed against his shoulder, but she did.

WHEN THE REST of the student population came flooding back to campus, Emiko felt oddly disappointed. Her weeks off with Drew and their nearly constant togetherness and training had been wonderful.

But it was time to get back to academics, and rededicate herself to being first in her graduating class.

She'd happily let Drew be second.

She threw herself into physics, math, diplomacy, and flight training. Instead of seeing Drew every day, she saw him four or five times a week. She'd expected to see a lot less of him since their academic paths were diverging more, but it worked out better than she'd expected.

Val and Jane, too, returned for their second year and worked hard to meet the renewed demands of their studies. Some faces Emiko had seen around campus had disappeared—they'd either graduated with the other third-years or washed out. New faces arrived, taking the place Emiko and her classmates had held a year ago.

Though she was only a year ahead of the newcomers, the disparity between her and them felt much greater.

Sometimes she wondered if her life as a PAC officer would be like that—prematurely aging her until she felt far older than a human could possibly live.

Nah. It wasn't like clandestine ops officers had a history of dying of old age. She'd fight until she couldn't fight anymore, and that would be it.

It was all she wanted, really.

Although she wouldn't mind getting to fight alongside Drew. She hoped they'd end up in the same department after OTS and their specialty schools.

Year Two of the academy marked the beginning of actual flight training, though they still used the simulators a great deal.

Interestingly, a few people washed out right away. Three went right after the first atmospheric puddle jumper flight. Two went after their first trip up an orbital elevator to do a turn around the station in a basic little class-one cruiser.

The only significant difference, in Emiko's opinion, was the fact that they knew they weren't safe inside a simulator. Real physics were working on their bodies, with real-life consequences if things went awry. When she lifted her little plane up off the tarmac, her body was actually rising higher and higher above the Earth's surface, and quickly reaching certain-death altitude.

That wasn't a technical term. It was just what her classmates called it when the professor wasn't around.

Fewer people in her class meant more flight time for her. She wasn't sorry to see the washouts go. She loved the tickle in her stomach when her aircraft left the planet's surface, and she loved the feeling of undocking a cruiser from the station, knowing there was nothing between her and the cold vacuum of space but a bit of technology and her skills.

It was exhilarating in a way that nothing else was.

Her love of flying made her wonder increasingly about what Drew's specialty was. Clearly, fighting would be a particular skill for him, but what else? What did he do that was special enough to get him recruited like she had been? Was there something he loved as much as she loved piloting?

One day when she was lying on his bed studying propulsion mechanics and he was at his desk, she blurted it out.

"What do you do better than anyone?"

He looked up, blinking. He'd apparently been deeply entrenched in his study because it took him a long moment for his expression to clear. He didn't even offer a suggestive response.

"What do you mean?" he asked.

"I fight. I fly. What got you here?" She was careful not to say more, and to let him answer in a way that didn't overtly say too much. It was the first time they'd broached the subject of why they were really there.

"I can hack anything. I can get into any system, and not leave a trace." His words weren't boastful. Merely factual.

She was surprised by how relieved she was that he'd answered. She'd crossed a line they'd never crossed, and it was dangerous. She wondered if he might refuse to answer.

"Show me," she said.

His eyebrows lifted, but then he smiled. "Yeah?"

"Yeah." She got up and went to stand behind his shoulder.

He thought for a moment. "Okay. Watch."

He opened up a multitude of windows, typing in lines of code as he switched between windows. None of it meant anything to her.

Finally, he said, "There. Look."

She saw a security camera's view of the door to her room. "No way."

He nodded, glowing with pride. "Yep. And that's not even a fraction of what I can really get into."

"Wow. So pretty much, the academy had to either make you into an officer or lock you up forever." She moved around and sat in his lap.

He laughed, and she felt the vibration against her shoulder. "Kind of."

He put his arms around her and she leaned against him, glad to give her brain a brief rest.

"What about you?" he asked.

"What do you mean?"

"Show me something impressive."

She nudged him. "You've seen me fight."

"Yeah, I have. Show me something else. Wow me."

She leaned back to get a better look at his face. "Really?"

"Really."

She thought about what she could show him that might be impressive. "Well, there are two options."

"Both," he said immediately.

"What?"

"Show me both. I want to be super impressed. Like, a could-not-be-more-impressed kind of impressed. Don't miss any opportunities to really knock my socks off."

"What?" She leaned back to look at his feet, unsure what he was saying.

"Old saying. Read it in a book. Never mind. So, when can we do this super-impressive stunt show? I'm excited now."

"Well, one of them would be difficult to impossible on campus. So how about just the one, and if it fails to impress, we can figure out a way to do the other?"

"It'll do. Let's get started."

She laughed. "Tomorrow."

He looked disappointed. "Not now? I was kind of hoping for now. This topology work is kicking my ass."

She gave him a quick peck and stood. "Sorry. Homework first. Tomorrow, I'll take your shoes off."

"Knock my socks off," he corrected.

"Whatever. Just know that tomorrow, you will have no footwear at all."

"That's not what it means," he sighed, pretending to be aggrieved.

"Just do your math," she told him.

THE NEXT DAY, after running in the morning, a full day of classes, and a training session with Drew and Whelkin, Emiko got everything together to give Drew a good impressing he wouldn't soon forget.

She hoped.

"Ready?" She pushed a black bag into his arms as soon as he came into her room.

"Almost." He set the bag down. "Let's go get Val and Jane."

"I'm not sure that's a good idea." She was wary of showing them too much of what she was capable of.

"Why? Are you going to be killing someone with your bare hands?"

"No. No killing."

He rubbed his chin in faux contemplation. "Hm. Will you be breaking any laws?"

"No."

"Will you be wearing chartreuse?"

"No. Why?" She zipped up her backpack.

"I just don't think it would be a good color on you."

She laughed. "Well, no. None of that."

"Then we're in the clear, I think. We don't have to pretend we don't have any skills, or that we aren't exceptional. We just have to be cool about how we might use those skills someday."

"Right." And he *was* right. The more intensive her schooling became, the more important it became for them to have something recreational to let off some of the pressure. "Okay, we'll ask them on the way. Grab that bag."

Val and Jane were instantly intrigued, and agreed to come along for what Drew promised to be a "spectacular showing of bravery and skill."

She didn't know about showing bravery, but she was about to show off all kinds of skill.

She'd prepared their basement dojo ahead of time, so when they entered, they all saw the large targets she'd set up against the back wall.

"Oooh." Jane clapped her hands. "I don't know what this is, but it's going to be good."

Emiko took off her backpack and slid a bandolier, heavy with knives, over her shoulders and snapped it into place. Then she put a belt around her waist and slid more knives into it.

She sneaked a peek at Drew. He was playing it cool, but his right eyebrow had raised ever so slightly, telling her he was, in fact, deeply intrigued.

"You've done this before, right?" he asked. "You're not, like, giving this a whirl for the first time right now?"

She smirked at him, then pointed. "If you don't mind, could you all stand over there?"

They did as asked, and she lined herself up against the large target. It was square, with concentric circles leading inward to the bullseye. She steadied the harness with her right hand to ensure it wouldn't shift, then in rapid succession, threw three knives.

Thunk, thunk, thunk.

They landed just left of the center of the target, dead center, and just to the right, in perfect intervals, with the blades oriented at precisely the same angles.

Val and Jane cheered and clapped.

Drew's eyebrow lifted another centimeter, as did one corner of his mouth.

She retrieved the three knives, replacing them into the bandolier, then returned to her previous position.

This time, she threw two knives to the top of a circle, threw another two at the bottom, and followed up with one of the longer knives from her belt buried dead center.

She'd created a perfect square, then put the last knife in the middle.

Val and Jane broke out into more applause.

"Wow!" Val exclaimed.

Emiko retrieved the knives.

"Got any trick shots?" Drew asked.

"There are no trick shots in knife throwing. Only accurate throws and inaccurate throws."

"So, you can't do something like throw knives with a blindfold?"

She shrugged. "I could try."

Val and Jane exchanged a wary look.

"Why not?" Drew asked. "Sounds fun."

"Okay. Do you have a blindfold?"

"I have my socks," he said. "They're still on my feet."

"I am not putting your sock anywhere near my face."

He sighed dramatically. "Okay, let's see." His eyes fell on Jane. "Your headband! That would work."

Jane asked, "You want my headband?"

"If you please." Drew gave her his most charming smile.

She pulled it off, still looking dubious.

He settled the cloth over Emiko's eyes. "You can't see, can you?"

"Nope."

"Okay, then." He moved away.

"Are you clear?"

"Fire away," he said.

The trick to throwing blind was to keep her feet and chin exactly in the same place. Move them the slightest bit, and it was all over. In her mind, she pictured the large center target and the smaller one to each side.

She pulled one of the longer knives from her belt and threw it at the center target, then whipped out a pair of the smaller ones and threw them simultaneously at the smaller ones.

From the reaction of squeals, laughter, and clapping, she determined she'd succeeded even before she removed the headband from over her eyes.

Each knife stabbed into the center of a target.

"Tada." She bowed.

"I dunno," Drew said. "That was pretty awesome, but my socks are still on. Don't you have something super showy, like to impress people at competitions or something?"

"Well, there is this one thing. It's kind of dangerous, though."

"Ooooh, dangerous." Drew grinned. "Let's definitely do that."

She looked to Val and Jane, who shrugged and nodded. By this time, it seemed, they were convinced that she wouldn't stab their eyes out.

"All right. Move to the back corner, please, just in case." She didn't anticipate anything going wrong, and the only person really in danger would be herself. But she'd done this thousands of times and had no worries.

She removed the bandolier and the belt, and gripped a smaller knife in each hand.

She backed up to the furthest point of the opposite wall, then took two running steps, reached for the floor with her closed fists to execute a cartwheel, then did a tucked front flip. As she rotated, as soon as she got her eyes on the target, she snapped her hands forward, landing on her feet as the knives slammed into the target.

Both right in the center.

Her audience of three cheered and applauded

Drew bent down, removed his shoes, peeled off his socks, and waved them like flags of surrender. "My socks are yours, my lady, and fairly won."

"Keep your socks," Emiko said. "Tomorrow you can buy me lunch. A really good one."

"Okay. But wait. What's in the bag?" He reached for the bag he'd carried for her.

"Just some shabby clothes that need to be recycled."

"Why make me carry it?"

"It seemed funny."

They all laughed.

After doing some more throws to entertain her friends, they headed back to their room.

On the way, they talked, teased, and continued laughing. It was nice. And when Val and Jane asked them if they wanted to come to their room for a drink and some Bennite card game she'd never heard of, she was actually regretful to have to say no.

"Another night," she promised. "I have an exam coming up on Kanaran culture and history, and it's not going to be easy."

It was nice to have a little group of friends who not only didn't mind her quirks, but liked the unique things that made her different.

"Should I go?" Drew asked after closing the door of her room behind him.

"Do you have something you can work on?"

"Always."

"Then stay. If you want to." She liked him being nearby, even when they were working on different things.

THE NIGHT of Emiko's knife throwing demonstration, they studied for hours. Rather than going back to his room, an exhausted Drew slept in her room.

From that point on, though, it became more and more common for her to sleep at his dorm, or for him to sleep at hers. Halfway through their second year, he moved into her room with her. They'd both turned eighteen already, and nobody would care.

Emiko liked having his things mixed in with hers. Not that he owned more than she did. Even though the room was only meant for one person, it worked just fine for them.

Right around that same time, Whelkin, who had previously seemed satisfied with her efforts and progress, suddenly seemed displeased with her efforts. He pushed her much harder than before. They met in her basement dojo and trained for hours. By the end, she felt like jelly. Like bruised and battered jelly.

He hit harder, and berated her when she failed to block or evade.

"Again," he'd say, even as the side of her face felt like it had been caved in. "This time, don't bend your elbow."

She'd do it again, as many times as he demanded, but he never had a word of praise for her. He always seemed disappointed in her.

At the infirmary, she was regularly treated for sprains, along with the occasional cracked rib or fractured extremity.

He was harder on her when they worked one on one, but Drew had also noticed the change during their lessons together. He mentioned it to her once, with cautious concern, and they didn't speak about it again.

She felt like saying anything to complain would be admitting she wasn't cut out for what she wanted to do. Instead, she endured, and did her best to live up to Whelkin's increased expectations.

So far, it wasn't working. He seemed dissatisfied when they began a one-on-one lesson, and only became more so as they went along. When a stomach punch dropped her to her knees, Whelkin shook his head.

"I think we're done here, until you can get yourself together."

She sat up, feeling like her guts had been reduced to pudding. "What do you mean?"

"I mean I'm not going to train you again until you've shown you're going to step up. You might have won competitions before you got here, but there are no rules in the real world. No one to call a foul, no one to step in if things get too hard."

He squatted down beside her. "You know what happens in the world you're aiming for when you can't do your job? You die. And you get your team killed. Maybe a lot of innocent people, too. All because you weren't good enough."

He stood. "Maybe you should think about getting serious about a career in security. You'd be good enough for that."

"No!" She struggled to her feet. "I'll get better."

"Will you? Can you? You're small. Not strong enough. Not fast enough. If you can't overpower someone, you have to either outsmart them or be so fast they can't get you. I'm working with a brawler right now who would crack you in half like a toothpick if he got his hands on you. And he's not even an officer yet. What would you do against fully trained officers and mercenaries?"

"I'll work harder. I'll weight train. I'll be strong enough and fast enough. I'm not going to quit."

He sighed, shaking his head slowly. "You've got two months. If I don't see any improvement, I'll have you removed from the candidate list."

He wouldn't train her for two months? Missing eight weeks of training felt like a momentous loss. On the other hand, having only eight weeks to gain muscle mass and prove that she was strong enough seemed like hardly any time.

"I'll improve," she vowed.

He shrugged, as if it didn't matter to him, then grabbed his bag and left.

She leaned against the wall, then slid down it and ran her hands over her face.

What had just happened? Was she really falling short or was this some sort of test? Either way, she had to put everything she had into the next eight weeks of training.

She mentally calculated her academic load and cross-referenced it against workout time.

She'd cut out her morning runs. No more cardio. She'd increase her caloric intake, with special attention on protein and muscle-building enzymes. Maybe Jane and Val would have some additional dietary suggestions.

If she ate protein bars and nutritional supplement packets between classes, she could skip lunch and get in a second weight training session. She could do a third in the evening, then finish out the day with her academics.

It could work.

It had to.

4

Emiko woke, threw herself out of bed, and immediately opened a protein pack and stuffed it into her mouth as she dressed in workout clothes.

She secured her hair back in its customary little ponytail, then sat and picked up the dermal injector she'd put next to her bed the night before, alongside the protein pack and a mini pack of nutritive biogel.

The injector was easy to use. She lined it up with the crook of her arm and activated it, sending muscle-building compounds and enzymes into her bloodstream, along with a low dose of synthetic hormones.

All legal and aboveboard, Val and Jane had assured her. The two had taken great pleasure in devising her plan for nutrition and supplementing for rapid muscle growth. They'd taken her on for a special project in one of their classes, and intended to use the experience to position themselves at the top of their class.

Emiko was glad that her friends were so ambitious. Maybe that was why she got along with them. But she was even more glad they could help her achieve her goal. Because when all else was stripped away, nothing but her goal mattered.

She was three weeks into her eight-week interim and seeing modest gains. Every morning she woke up, assessed her body, and jumped into action. Her arms and chest constantly felt sore, but that wasn't a negative. It meant progress, and she was glad to feel those twinges and aches. She imagined her muscle fibers tearing, repairing themselves, and getting bigger. Stronger.

She grabbed her two prepacked bags, and bolted out the door.

At the gym, she utilized her time carefully. She executed compound movements to engage multiple muscle groups in her exercises.

She changed her routine every two days, never letting her body get accustomed to the workout. She pushed, doing everything that felt awkward, hard, and uncomfortable.

By the time her body felt like melted rubber, her time was up. She hit the shower room, getting clean and putting on fresh clothes, then headed for her first class, slurping down another nutritive biogel pouch for hydration and proper blood chemistry along with the whole-food supplement bars Jane and Val had prescribed for her.

They tasted less than delicious, but that didn't matter.

At least she could sit still in class and let her brain take over while her body recovered. She always felt stiff when she got up at the end of the first class, but she loosened up on the way to the next one, eating and drinking as she went.

At midday, she went back to the gym, then continued with the rest of her classes.

After her last class, she spent an hour in the library, getting a start on her homework for that day. Then she returned to the gym for her most grueling workout of the day.

Afterward, she sat on a bench in the shower room, digging deep to find the energy to get back to her dorm. She used a dermal injector to administer a small dose of just enough stimulant to get her through the rest of the day. That, too, had been approved by her personal healthcare duo. And bless them for it.

She dragged herself to her dorm. Drew wasn't there. Odd, since his classes were done for the day. He might have met up with friends, or maybe with classmates to work on something.

She hoped he was having more fun than she was.

Not that fun was important. She wasn't at the academy for fun. She came here to work, and to be the best.

She was a little sorry to go to bed alone, though. She thought about sending him a goodnight message, but didn't want to seem clingy. Neither of them liked that. They still didn't define themselves like other campus couples did. They just fit together, that was all. Being together made sense.

She pulled the blanket up to her chin and embraced the bliss of sleep.

EMIKO WOKE to Drew's slow breathing in her ear. How he'd managed to climb into the narrow bed without waking her, she didn't know. She was usually a light sleeper, but maybe her exhaustion had blunted that. Just as well.

She stole a minute to herself before getting up, tracing the shape of his earlobe with her fingertip. Then she rested her hand on his chest to feel the steady thumping of his heart.

Then she threw herself into her daily routine, just as she had the day before, and the day before that.

Halfway through her eight-week struggle, she wasn't seeing much of Drew, or attending meetings of the dinner club or holovid group. She just didn't have any time or energy to spare. Val clucked over her like a mother hen while she looked after Emiko's wounds. To her credit, and Jane's, too, they didn't berate her for treating her body so badly. They trusted her to do what she felt she needed to.

"Do you have a lot of projects going on?" she asked Drew one evening when they were both in her room, getting ready for bed. "I've missed seeing you."

"I do, but mostly I don't want to get in your way." He pulled his pajama shirt over his head and she felt a pang of regret that she was too damn exhausted to do anything more than appreciate the sight of him.

"You're never in my way." She made sure her bags were ready for the morning, and set out her injection, biogel, and protein pack next to the bed.

"I like hearing that." He lay down on the bed and held his arm up so she could lie against his chest with his arm around her.

"Then I'll say it again. You're never in my way. In fact, seeing you helps keep me extra motivated."

Instead of tickling her ear or saying something teasing, he sighed. "Look, I get that you need to do what you're doing. I respect how hard you're working. But the truth is, it isn't easy to see someone I care about tearing herself to shreds."

"Oh." She hadn't thought about it that way. She knew she didn't look good. She had circles under her eyes and, by the time she got back in the evenings, was often slumped over with fatigue and soreness. "I'm sorry."

He sighed again. "Don't be. You're doing what you need to do, and I'm behind you on it. I've missed you, but that doesn't matter because neither one of us came here to be in a relationship. I'm proud of how dedicated you are, but I don't take it personally. And I hope you won't take it personally if I work on my own things to keep myself focused on what I need to do rather than worrying about you."

"No, you're right. I hadn't thought about it from your perspective, but I get it. The further we get in our careers, the more they'll probably pull us apart. I mean, it pushes us together, because of what we have in common, but..." she trailed off, finding it difficult to make her point.

"But we'll be under unusual stress, and it will have its effect."

"Yeah. It might put us at odds, and we'll have to deal with that." After school, they might be assigned to entirely different sectors of the galaxy, or one of them might go deep undercover.

He patted her shoulder. "We'll figure things out as we go along. For now, we'll each just focus on what we need to do. Deal?"

"Deal." She didn't like this conversation. It made her think about how hard it was to imagine her future without him, and how unlikely it was for him to be in it.

He kissed the top of her head. "Go to sleep. You have a lot to do tomorrow."

SIX WEEKS into her bulking-up endeavor, she could see and feel a difference. She could lift much heavier weights, and she saw a difference in her body, which was kind of a big thing. People from her genetic background did not put on muscle mass easily. A person could be super strong, but look downright skinny. Seeing a physical difference gave her hope.

She kept on with the weight training, and added martial arts practice in the evenings. This meant less sleep, and less attention on her academic studies. She'd slip in her classes, but it was a calculated risk. In two weeks, once Whelkin evaluated her, she could throw herself back into her studies and catch up. She had to make the sacrifice now, though, for her long-term best interest.

Drew showed up less and less often. She supposed she must look terrible, and he probably preferred to sleep in his old dorm rather than see the toll her efforts were taking.

It was for the best, but she missed him.

One day shy of the eight-week mark, she returned to her dojo to find Whelkin sitting in the chair behind the desk. It was odd to see him there, in the space she and Drew had made into a training room. She wasn't surprised Whelkin knew about it, though. He probably knew everything about her life on campus.

"Ready?" He lounged in the chair, as if they were having a casual social visit.

Was she? She felt exhausted and stretched thin. She'd thought she'd fall into bed, but instead she had to fight for the life she wanted. All she could do was say, "Yes."

Whelkin stood. "Let's go."

In their basement dojo, they circled each other. She thanked her body chemistry for the boost of adrenaline that surged through her. She felt her exhaustion underneath it, but she'd ride the wave for as long as she could.

Be faster, Whelkin had said. *Be stronger. Fight smarter.*

She'd had eight weeks to think about how to beat him. Eight weeks to analyze his style, cross-reference it against his teaching style, and again by his lesson content.

She'd also analyzed her own style, and what he would expect from her. And she'd spent her time developing and training techniques he wouldn't expect.

Fight smarter. Be stronger. That's what she'd do.

She began as she would have before, in a judo stance, waiting to see what he would spring on her. But before he could launch his attack, she moved in under his guard, unleashed an uppercut, and grappled him to the ground. Before he had time to overpower her, she went for the kill shot, punching him in the trachea.

She pulled the punch, delivering it with only a fraction of its power so as not to actually harm him. But she'd proved herself. Within three seconds of his test, she'd already shown him everything he needed to know about her.

He couldn't make her give up. No matter what his complaint was, she'd find a way to get better.

She stood, backed up, and barked, "Again!" just as he did when they were training.

She couldn't take him by surprise twice, but she fought hard, changed up her tactics, and did everything she could to show him how she could use her strength and her smarts to win.

Be stronger. Fight smarter.

Five minutes in, she realized with shock that he was truly fighting her. He wasn't just poking at her, testing her skills. He was giving her his best.

And she was still standing.

Prelin's ass!

A rush of success consumed her, and she threw the extra energy into her attack. Strike, shove, block, kick, dodge, throw. And again. And again.

"Enough!" Whelkin shouted. He didn't let down his guard until she dropped her arms and stepped back, breathing hard.

She felt like a monster. A god. She was made of pure energy and the desire to win. She burned to keep fighting.

"Get hold of yourself, recruit. Control it." He glared at her.

He knew the euphoria she was feeling. That fact made her pull herself up hard and try to get a grip.

It wasn't easy. She paced, swinging her arms out, imagining the aggression leaking out of her.

"Now sit." He said it so commandingly that the part of herself that was still hopped-up on killer instinct wanted to rebel.

She sat.

"Good. Take two rest days, then we start fresh. From now on, every time we train, bring this with you."

She felt no wave of relief or triumph. She'd known she'd passed the test when she realized he was fighting her full-out.

"Was this about finding the berserker within, or about seeing how far I'd go to succeed?" She folded her hands in her lap.

"Both. If you want to make it, you have to be able to devote yourself to a singular purpose and do whatever it takes to achieve it. That'll be your job. You have to be smarter, harder, and tougher than anyone else. Anyone. Even me." He stared at her, unblinking.

"Why am I getting this lesson now? Why not months ago, or next year?"

"Because you weren't ready before. You were too controlled. Too distant. And because if you didn't start now, it would be too late. You're up against some hard competition, and you have to be able to beat all of them."

"Why? Will there be only one selected from my class?" Her mind went to Drew.

"No. There will be four. One team. That's it. But you can't be just one of the four. You have to be the best, because you were recruited to lead."

"So either I become the leader or I don't make it at all?" She tried to understand the reasoning.

"Each class has a select handful of potentials for special ops, carefully chosen for their diversity of skills to operate as a team. If you aren't selected as a leader, there's no space for you."

"I have no choice but to be number one." It had always been her aim, but in the back of her mind, she'd thought that being one of the top few would qualify her.

"In two days, we begin your real training. Every day, just like this. Be ready. And be sure this is what you really want." Whelkin stood. Apparently, they were done here.

She walked slowly back to her room. A deep conflict pulled her insides in opposing directions. On the one hand, she'd broken through a threshold, and she'd qualified for some real truths from Whelkin. And she'd passed his test. On the other, she felt a new burden.

She had to be the best. She had to do everything she could to beat Drew, no matter what that meant for him.

For the second time that day, when she opened the door to what she'd expected to be an empty room, someone was there to greet her. This time, it was Drew, and Emiko could not have been more glad.

Her senses still thrummed from earlier, and adrenaline still zinged through her veins. The world felt more vibrant and alive and...no, *she* felt more alive. Most of the time, she lived in a middle ground of calculated expectation. Her mood neither rose too far above the baseline, nor sank too far below it.

But now, she felt fantastically free and wild and full of many different emotions.

"Wow," Drew said, leaning forward to put his elbows on his knees. "So, you failed, huh?"

"What makes you think I took the test?" He had known something about it beforehand? It was funny how commonplace she now found it to question what people knew, and how normal she found it to assume that she was always being watched and listened to.

"You're sort of glowing," he said, painting a shape around her with his hands. "Like a star."

"I *am* a star," she agreed. "Someday, I'm going to rule this whole place."

Not really. Her intended profession didn't work that way. But it was fun to say.

"Yeah, you are." He reached out, and, when she gave him her hand, he tugged her down into his lap. "Admiral Emiko."

"I'll make sure you get an admiralty, too," she promised. "Otherwise it would just kind of be weird, you know?"

He tilted her back and tickled her mercilessly.

That touched off a whole tickle war, which led to a pillow fight, which segued into other, less combative pursuits.

IN THE MORNING, Drew got up bright and early and dressed for a run. "Are we running together again or are you still bulking up?"

"I'll go back to running in two days. I'm giving my body a rest, then I'll get right back to it.. Why, do you not like my new muscles?" She struck a bodybuilding pose, which was silly since she'd never actually become bulky without some unhealthy interventions.

"No, I like them a lot. They're very womanly."

She squinted at him, trying to decide if he was teasing. It was hard to tell with him sometimes.

"I mean it," he insisted. "You look great."

"Well, good then." She rolled onto her side. "Now you go for a run, and I'm going to treat myself to another hour of sleep before I throw myself into catching up on my classes."

"You got it. Sweet dreams." He closed the door quietly behind him.

EMIKO FINISHED out the second year of the academy with a vengeance. Her sessions with Whelkin became absolutely brutal. It wasn't unusual for one or both of them to break a bone or two, though they immediately went to the infirmary to have them healed.

Whelkin rarely trained her and Drew together. She didn't know why, and he didn't answer when she asked.

She didn't ask a second time. Not everything was hers to know yet.

She saw less of Drew because her weekends kept her off campus, doing flight training. Finally, she got to actually be in a ship. It felt like it had taken forever.

They ran together every morning she was on campus, though, and fit in weight training when they could. She was determined to keep building her strength. Whelkin clearly thought she'd need it.

The run-up to the end of the year was nearly frantic. Emiko and Drew had no time for picnics on the quad or watching a holo-vid with Jane and Val. Every minute of their waking hours was accounted for. She even skipped the group activities she carefully attended to maintain her appearance of being a well-rounded student.

Drew began to struggle with something. She didn't know what it was, but she watched the shadows under his eyes grow. He always kept up his good spirits, but sometimes he was too exhausted for anything but sleep.

"Is something going on?" she asked one night when they were both studying late. She suspected that when she went to sleep, he'd keep working. He'd been doing that a lot lately.

"Yeah. Kind of. I can't talk about it, though."

"Oh." She tried to think what that could mean. "So, it's like what I went through with Whelkin, but for your specialty?"

"More or less. Can we stop talking about it, though?" He looked uncharacteristically anxious.

"Of course. Sorry."

"Don't be. This is just part of it all." He gave her a small smile, then returned his attention to the voicecom screen.

Times like that reminded her of why they never called each other things like "boyfriend" or "girlfriend." They rarely spoke of their feelings, either. They were nothing like other couples.

Absolutely nothing.

WHEN HER THIRD year of the academy began, Emiko felt so much older than she'd been the day she arrived on campus. The incoming class, even those already older than her, seemed like naïve children. She was fast becoming aware of some of the hard truths of the universe, and learning to second-guess everything.

The beginning of the year touched off a new ferocity to her training. She suffered concussions, broken arms, and torn ligaments every week. She had a particular doctor assigned to her, and got to know him well.

Meanwhile, her academic schoolwork shifted to specific aspects of diplomacy, law, and intensive flight training.

Despite the pain and injury, she felt like a propulsion chamber finally getting up to full speed. She felt everything more intensely than she ever had before—both the highs and the lows. Adrenaline became a normal part of her daily routine, and she thrived on it.

Whelkin pushed her harder than ever before. He berated every mistake.

"You're dead!" he'd shout at her when she made a mistake.

"There's a brawler you're competing against who is going to rip you limb from limb if you don't step it up! Then he'll get your place at OTS and you can go be a security babysitter for the rest of your life."

Every time he berated her, she leaped back to her feet, ready to go again. To do it better. To fight smarter, and get stronger. His criticisms only motivated her. She saw them as nothing but attempts to weed out a weak candidate.

That wasn't her.

Then one day, three months into her third year, she felt a shift in her combat abilities. She arrived at a level of skill that made things she'd struggled with feel natural. Like they were no effort at all.

She felt it in her body as she dodged, twisted, and struck back at Whelkin. What had once required so much effort now came instinctively, as a reflex. Like the time she had demonstrated her bo staff skills to Drew, her brain was so hardwired with skill it seemed her body was acting on its own.

In a beautiful ballet of murder, she slipped in under Whelkin's attacks, threw him over her hip, and followed him to the ground, her hands on his throat and adrenaline roaring in her ears.

They froze that way, eyes locked, for a long moment.

"You're dead," she said evenly, repeating back the words he'd said to her so often. "You'll never beat me again."

From that point on, he never did. She learned to win even with a broken arm or only one eye that worked right.

It was brutal, it was vicious, and it was everything.

She wished she could tell Drew about her success, but there were more things than ever she couldn't discuss with him. No doubt he'd had successes he couldn't tell her about, too.

Their isolation, ironically, only strengthened the bond between them, because they both understood it.

Their feelings for one another grew deeply intense. She had a hard time doing things in moderation, and Drew was the same. It was yet another thing they had in common.

She could practically see him growing taller and more muscular. His boyishness had melted away, and been replaced with more of an edge.

He was her competition, and they had to keep secrets from each other, but she felt like he was the only person in her life who could truly understand her.

Drew was her best friend, her lover, and her partner on this quest. His teasing and occasional whimsy kept her grounded into life. She wondered if, without him, she might become nothing but a killing machine.

Finally, four months into their third year, he nailed the backflip, surprising them both.

When he landed on his feet, rather than on his knees or a combination of his feet and hands, he wore such a look of shock that Emiko laughed.

"Woo!" he shouted in triumph, sweeping her up in a hug and spinning her around. "I did it! Yes!"

"Quick, do it again, before you forget how," she prompted.

They spent the rest of their free time doing backflips. Drew didn't land them all, but he succeeded more often than he didn't.

They were both making strides.

It was all coming together, and she could envision her future more clearly than ever. She felt so close to being able to grasp it within her fingers.

Lying in bed that night, after her mind had gone hazy with sleep, Drew spoke softly in her ear.

"I feel like something's about to happen."

The sleep haze lifted slightly, but she didn't open her eyes. "Like what?"

"I don't know. It's just a feeling I have sometimes, like when a storm is building. Skies have gone gray, the wind has picked up, and you're just waiting for the clouds to open up and drench you. You ever get that?"

"No." She wanted to keep talking to him, but she began to drift off again.

"Something's coming," he murmured. "I feel it."

"Go to sleep." Her words were slurred with fatigue. "If the boogeyman comes, I'll protect you."

He chuckled and kissed the top of her head. "Okay, let's sleep."

He was right, though. Something was coming.

EMIKO ALWAYS APPROACHED flight training with absolute delight. It didn't matter if it was hand-calculating vectors or weight loads or actually flying. She loved it all.

Especially the flying. As she took her seat in the classroom, she wondered what they'd be doing that day. Simulators, probably.

When her instructor, Captain Martinez, entered wearing a flight suit, Emiko perked up.

"I have good news and bad news today," Martinez said. She was a fit woman in her forties, with short brown hair and an odd sense of humor.

Emiko liked her.

"The bad news is that some of you have come as far as you're going to in the flight program. If you're still here, that means you've been rated for small atmospheric crafts and cruisers up through class four. So, congratulations on that—those PAC flight ratings are hard to come by." Martinez looked slowly around the room.

Emiko remained still, but she heard others shifting around nervously.

"If I call your name, the good news is that you will now have additional time to focus on your other studies. The final six months of the academy are notorious for their difficulty, which is why we thin out the flight program at this point." Martinez recited name after name. Most did not surprise Emiko, but a few students shuffled out with obvious disappointment.

What did surprise her was that in the end, only she and one other remained.

Martinez smiled at them. "Congratulations, Emiko and Belen."

They looked at each other. Belen was an intense Bennite she barely knew. He kept to himself, though she'd been curious about him. He wasn't pursuing medicine, which made him unusual among his people.

Every planet needed a complement of all professions, including pilots, but unusual people interested her. However, he'd struck down any attempts at friendliness from anyone.

Emiko had had to find out what little she knew about him via the voicecom.

She wondered if he might be competition for clandestine ops.

"I have good news and bad news for you, too," Martinez continued. "You'll be doing your first atmospheric launches today."

Emiko contained herself with great effort. It wasn't easy to hide the elation filling her chest like a balloon behind a mask of indifference.

She was still working on that.

"Will we be co-piloting with someone?" Belen asked.

"Here's the thing about atmospheric launches," Martinez said. "You've both launched via the simulators hundreds of times. Even when malfunctions and errors are intentionally created, you handled them as well as any experienced pilot. At this point, there is nothing for you to learn from shadowing someone else. You'll each be piloting your own vessel."

Should Emiko feel nervous about that? She dug deep, looking for a sense of foreboding, but didn't find it. She felt only the sweet singing of adrenaline running through her veins.

Still, she hid all of that behind a mask of indifference.

"I'm glad to see you're pleased." Martinez looked amused.

Damn. Clearly, Emiko still needed to work at being inscrutable.

"So that's it for now," their teacher concluded. "Go change into your flight suits, pack an overnight bag with everything you'll need for the weekend, and meet at the launchpad in three hours. Dismissed."

Emiko steeled herself to walk normally when she really ached to run.

A solo atmospheric launch. This was huge.

She couldn't wait.

EMIKO ATE a quick lunch in her room as she packed and changed, hoping to maximize her time there so she might see Drew before she left. No luck, though. He was used to her having weekend flight training, so he wouldn't be too surprised to find her gone.

She left him a message on the voicecom and a handwritten note, which amused her. Notes to him were the only thing she wrote out by hand. Something about it was just more personal than a message on the voicecom.

Sometimes she drew a picture for him, too. In her opinion, her utter lack of artistic skill made her drawings endearing.

She tried to sketch a ship, but it looked more like a rock. She tried adding some lines beneath it, to suggest propulsion, but that made it look more like a faucet pouring water.

It was the thought that counted.

She hopped a tram to take her to the launchpad, a full hour away from campus. She wondered at the launch procedure to come. Atmospheric flights needed a lot of thrust to escape the atmosphere, so they couldn't just set up two ships side by side. Maybe they had a remote location for a second launch, or maybe she and Belen would take off on different days.

The details didn't matter. She was thrilled to be going on this adventure, no matter what shape it might take.

She had to admit that, as she walked into the flight command center, wearing her flight suit and knowing she was about to launch into space, she felt pretty badass. This was a moment she'd dreamed of her whole life. She savored every step.

It wasn't every day a dream finally came true.

At the reception desk, she gave her name along with that of Captain Martinez. A stern young man escorted her down a short hall to what appeared to be a meeting room.

Captain Martinez was already inside, but the student sitting next to her wasn't Belen.

It was Drew.

When he looked up to see her, his expression of surprise felt like a mirror of her own reaction.

Emiko said nothing. She bowed deeply to Martinez in deference to her rank, and gave the shallow bow of a fellow student to Drew. Then she sat, waiting for answers.

Martinez cleared her throat. "You've no doubt guessed that this isn't just a training mission. The two of you have been paired to see how you work together, as well as how you perform your essential duties."

Emiko eyed Drew, wondering exactly what his function on this mission would be. His expression was guarded, but she knew him well enough to see him sorting through his own suspicions.

They were both wondering if this was a head-to-head competition to get into the clandestine ops division.

If so, it didn't matter. She'd do her best, he'd do his best, and the rest would be out of their hands.

She should play it cool. Be respectful. This was her chance to show Martinez and PAC command how professional she could be as an officer.

But a glow was growing within her. Adrenaline combined with ambition and a desire to push all of her limits.

She grinned at Drew. "Let's do this."

He broke into a broad grin of his own. "Absolutely."

She felt like the world was expanding around her, to accommodate her growing hunger for adventure, and the sense she and Drew were a pairing that just couldn't lose.

She looked to Captain Martinez, expecting a look of mild disdain or disapproval.

Instead, she saw...satisfaction.

Well. Prelin's ass. It seemed like she was succeeding already. Wisely, though, she kept her mouth shut and waited to see what came next.

Martinez arched an eyebrow at them. "Your mission is to go to Luna, infiltrate the branch academy office there, and return with all of the internal correspondence that has been sent there for the last three days, at all classification levels."

Emiko struggled not to look at Drew and to keep her expression guarded. Both took great effort.

"Are they aware of this?" she asked.

"Does it matter?" Martinez fired back. "Whether it's a real mission or just a training exercise, do the stakes change?"

"Objectively, no," Drew answered. "Though it would be nice to know if we're up against an actual threat of bodily harm."

"Assume you are. Always assume you're up against a life-and-death situation."

Emiko looked down at her hands, folded very business-like on the conference table. Martinez was right. She had to approach everything in life as a life-and-death situation from this point on.

Her eyes finally met Drew's, and she knew he was down for this.

Oh, this was going to be good.

"You're sure you can fly one of these, right?" Drew's joking attitude struck Emiko as entirely appropriate. They'd reached a point of adrenaline-charged readiness that only humor put the brakes on the mania that threatened to claim them.

Well, at least her, anyway. She could only assume he felt the same way.

She went through the pre-launch checklist, ticking one thing after another off. It felt so right, and so natural. She'd wondered if she'd have jitters about doing this for real, on her own, but she didn't.

She was ready to go.

Finally, the countdown came.

"Should I be scared?" Drew joked again.

She looked over at him and grinned. He was very cute

wearing a flight headset. "Terrified. I think I forgot something. Pretty sure we're going to die."

She hadn't forgotten a thing, but his laugh was a worthy reward.

Three...two...one...

"If you haven't done one of these," she said, "you might want to brace yourself."

Engage.

Prelin's ass, she was doing it. A fireball lit underneath them, providing the initial thrust to throw them out of Earth's gravitational field. The sensation, though buffered through all the inertial dampening, felt much like having her skin peeled off her skeleton by the sheer onlay of force.

It was horrible, yet also fantastic. She held her breath. All training manuals said not to, but she'd found it necessary to counteract the pressure against her chest that made it impossible to breathe anyway.

She probably should have suggested that to Drew. Too late now.

Two thrilling minutes after launch, they cleared the exosphere, and she could breathe again.

Clearly, so could Drew, because he launched into a string of expletives that she'd never heard from him.

"You actually want to do that on a regular basis, on purpose?" he shouted.

She removed her headset, because he was about to deafen her. "We all do what we're good at. Don't worry. Atmospheric launches are rare, because ships that are capable of it are expensive and hard to come by. Plus, it eats up an enormous amount of fuel. Don't worry. You'll get your chance to show off the thing you're good at soon enough."

His wide-eyed look of outrage faded. "That makes me feel a little better. Though I doubt it will look like much to you. Mostly just keying stuff in. You might not know how impressed you should really be."

"That would be a shame." She smirked as she made a slight course correction and projected their arrival time.

"Huge," he agreed, pulling off his own headset. "A massive shame. I'd be like one of those great artists, unappreciated in my own time."

"Twelve hours to arrival. All systems optimal. We're in good shape." She communicated that information back to the control center, wondering how closely Martinez would follow their flight.

Not just Captain Martinez, though. She was certain that all the people pertinent to her entry into clandestine ops would be paying attention. She recognized that this was her final exam. A do-or-die test to see if she had what it took to do the job.

And Drew's final exam, too. Did that mean they were in direct competition, or that maybe they'd even get to work together?

She barely dared to hope.

They didn't discuss it, but he had to be thinking the same thing.

"Good." Drew removed his safety straps and slid out of his seat. Artificial gravity allowed him to walk normally to the back of the ship's cabin and sit at a science station.

As far as atmospheric ships went, this was the extra basic version. As small as possible, and with minimal amenities. Other than an access conduit beneath the deck plate, the ship was one cabin with multipurpose seats that would fold out into beds.

Not that she expected to sleep. All it would take was one moment of inattention for her future to go into the abyss. She wouldn't let that happen.

Besides, she doubted she could sleep even if she tried. She was too hopped up on the excitement of the adventure.

"What are you doing?" she asked Drew, as she scanned the space ahead for asteroids or debris. The ship's sensors should automatically alert her of such things based on their flight path, but she was leaving nothing to chance.

"Working on my part of all this." His head lifted from the console. "I guess I can tell you now, since we're working on this together."

That came as a small surprise for her, too. They'd been so guarded about their work before that it had become natural to avoid discussing specifics.

He continued, "I'm seeking out all access ports on Luna and testing their vulnerabilities. When I'm done with that, I'll start working on the specific nodes associated with the academy branch office, and monitoring their traffic."

"You can do that?"

He grinned. "That's just for starters. When we get closer, I'll take over some of the interfaces, including their own security system. Then we can monitor the inside of the office."

His smile slipped when he noticed her expression. "What?"

She returned to her own work. "Nothing. You just looked really hot to me, all of a sudden."

"More than usual?"

"Definitely."

"Hm." He sounded thoughtful. "Good to know. For what it's worth, you look awfully hot yourself, in the pilot's seat looking all official."

They grinned at each other like a pair of idiots.

She didn't care if PAC intelligence, or anyone else, was listening in at the moment. Their attraction to each other couldn't possibly be a secret to anyone who might be listening.

Was a big mission always like this?

She hoped so. She felt like she'd been sleepwalking through her whole life and she'd finally woken up.

THE INITIAL RUSH of excitement waned as the hours passed, but Emiko's overall high remained. Drew didn't talk much, since he was absorbed in his work. She kept herself busy checking and rechecking absolutely everything she could.

On one hand, she could hardly wait to arrive and do the job they'd been assigned. On the other, she didn't want this heightened sense of anticipation and adventure to end.

Prior to coming to the academy, she hadn't realized she was such a thrill-seeker. She'd always considered herself unusually serious.

Now here she was, piloting an atmospheric-launch-capable ship on a covert mission to the moon alongside the most attractive guy she'd ever known.

It was fantastic. One hundred percent pure joy.

When they moved in on Luna, Drew relayed the logistics of what they needed to do.

"Here's the deal. We're going to have to physically get into the office."

"Why?" She'd expected him to work some sort of electronic wizardry and just strip the data remotely.

"Because that's how this is set up. That's obviously the job they want us to do. A physical infiltration and hack."

"Tell me what you need." She didn't know the intricacies of what he did and would have to rely on him to handle those bits.

"I can get us past their security system, no problem. I can keep us off their security feeds. I hope to wipe out any evidence of my tampering, but I'll have to be inside their system to be able to do it. Our problem is the risk of being seen by real, living people. They're the main variable."

She nodded slowly, thinking. "Can you get into their personnel system? See who all is in the building?"

"Yes."

"Can you get the data for entries and exits, and personnel, for every day for the past two weeks? And all messages for the person who sits at the reception desk."

A slow smile slid across his face. "I see where you're going. Nice."

"I've been learning a thing or two in my security classes while you've been working on all this hacking stuff."

During the remaining three hours before arrival, they huddled together over the voicecom terminal, analyzing behavior patterns and looking for any indicators of abnormalities to the daily routine.

"Okay. Now can you program a sensor lock on each of these people? Then we can establish location parameters, and, if the people go outside of them, your program can alert our comports."

"I like it," he said. "Here, hand me your comport and I'll rig that up."

He held out his hand for her small portable voicecom unit.

By the time they began their approach to Luna, they had their plan in place.

5

"Oh, I didn't realize he'd be on vacation." Emiko bit her lip. "You don't think there'd be anyone else I could talk to, do you? He said he'd get back to me about my application."

She was glad she'd packed a simple black knee-length skirt and a smart white blouse. Not knowing what to expect, she'd tried to go as generically multi-occasion as possible.

"I'll check with the human resources department." The middle-aged woman at the desk gave her a reassuring smile. "Would you like to have a seat?"

"Sure. Thank you." She ducked her chin shyly.

Mr. Slivig in HR had gone on vacation the day before. It made for the perfect timing of a near miss, and the opportunity for Emiko to keep an eye on the receptionist, and any possible visitors to the building.

She chose a seat at the far end, where the camera wouldn't get a good view of her face. They'd have no reason to believe she was not, in fact, Miss Heszenko, come to see about her application for the supply management position.

Drew would have gotten in through a service entrance at the side and, hopefully, was proceeding to the server room.

Emiko fidgeted for a couple of minutes, then picked up an infoboard and flipped through some *Living a Happy Life on Luna* type journalism. After a few minutes, she put the infoboard down and sat, bouncing her knee.

"Miss Heszenko?" the woman called from the desk.

Emiko approached again, ducking her head nervously.

"Mr. Slivig's assistant checked your file, and said that your verifications and references have all come in. Mr. Slivig will contact you as soon as he gets back. We're sorry for the confusion."

"Oh, well that's good news. Thank you." She beamed with relief. "I'll look forward to hearing from him. Everyone I've met here seems really nice."

The receptionist liked that. "Thank you. I hope it goes well for you."

Emiko nodded, bowed, then turned toward the door. She spun back suddenly, as if she'd just thought of something. "Actually, do you have a necessary I could use? I have a long walk to get back to the tram station."

"Of course. I'll buzz you in." The receptionist reached over and unlocked the door to the inner sanctum. "First door on the right. It's unlocked."

"Thank you."

She entered the necessary, went into a stall, and pulled out her comport. No message from Drew. She hoped he'd hurry. He'd said he would only need a few minutes once he got into position, and then a couple more minutes to get back out of the building.

That presumed everything went according to plan.

She felt relieved that her ploy to visit the necessary had worked. If Drew needed assistance, she was now in a better position to provide it. But if she stayed inside for more than ten minutes, the receptionist would probably come looking for her.

Or worse, security would.

That left her standing in a necessary stall, watching the minutes tick by on her comport. It was unexpectedly dull and mundane in the midst of such an exciting endeavor.

At the eight-minute mark, she got the signal that he was clear. She left the stall, washed her hands, then casually walked back through the security door. It clicked behind her.

"Thanks again. Have a nice day," she called to the receptionist. Then she walked out and into the pressurized walkway system.

She took a circuitous route, ducking under security cameras where she could, to prevent her path being traced. Pausing, she checked her comport again.

Drew had arrived at the meet point.

She ducked around a corner, waited for a man to pass by, then peeled off her blouse to reveal a blue tank top beneath. Then she rolled up the waist of her skirt to make it into a miniskirt. Finally, she pulled her hair loose of its bun and ruffled it to make it as wavy and disheveled as she could.

She pulled a checkered shoulder bag out of the prim pocketbook she carried, which was otherwise empty. Then she stuffed everything into the bag and slung it casually over her shoulder.

Her stride went from tight and measured to loose and hip-swinging. Though men had taken little notice of her before, suddenly the eyes of most guys she passed now pulled toward her like she was magnetized.

She ignored them. She only had eyes for Drew, and when she saw him waiting for her on the tram platform, her heart leapt. They'd pulled it off. Almost. They just had to get back off the moon.

He grinned as she approached, looking her up and down. They'd decided that their cover would be two romantically inclined teens with eyes only for each other, but she didn't mind throwing herself into his arms one bit.

"I like this look on you," he murmured in her ear. "You should wear this more often."

"Never going to happen," she answered. Then she squealed and laughed when he picked her up and spun her around.

"You'll mess up my hair!" she protested, then batted him flirtatiously on the shoulder.

Around them, people ignored their youthful foolishness. Just as they should.

They continued their charade on the tram, teasing, laughing, snuggling in for a smooch every now and then. Acting like people expected two kids their age to act.

Pretending to be average nineteen-year-olds felt like an ironic thing to Emiko. It only highlighted how they were entirely unlike others.

A pang of sadness startled her. She'd always felt somewhat isolated from typical kids, but somehow, the isolation suddenly felt stark. In retrospect, it seemed a little sad. Wouldn't it have been nice to do all the normal things in life? Other people seemed to like it awfully well. She just wasn't made that way.

No one but Drew understood her at a gut-deep level, and no one else could understand her dedication to her goals.

It was a lonely feeling making her want to cling to him.

"What's wrong?" Drew's smile had slipped.

The tram jolted with a sudden deceleration, making her grab for the pole to get her balance. Drew already had one hand on it, and his other arm went around her waist.

The voicecom blared to life. *We are experiencing a minor power fluctuation. Do not be alarmed, and please maintain your current position.*

Passengers grumbled, sighed, or acted ambivalent. Such things were common on Luna.

But Emiko had a feeling in the pit of her stomach that started like a pinprick and quickly grew to consume her entire chest.

"Something's wrong." She said it softly, so no one else would hear.

"What?" Drew asked.

"We're at the wrong point on the line for a deceleration. We're too close to a magnet. It should be pulling us forward, even if the power is fluctuating. This isn't right."

"How do you know that?" he whispered.

"I had some time, so I studied Luna's schematics. And I've been watching the kilometer markers."

"And you memorized all the magnet placements?" he didn't sound disbelieving, just perplexed. She'd never shown him how good her memory was.

"Yes. Do you trust me?" she stared up at him.

"I do." He didn't hesitate, and his eyes showed no doubt.

She took his hand. "We need to run."

She slammed her hand on the emergency button and forced the tram doors to open outward. She leaped out to the narrow service platform with Drew immediately following.

"What now?" he asked.

She took off to the right. "This way. Be careful!"

With little clearance between the tram and the wall, the ledge was not only narrow, but so was the space to fit their bodies. She managed well enough, but she knew that, behind her, Drew had to be having a harder time. He'd grown very broad-shouldered over the last couple years.

She waited for him to ask if she was just being paranoid, because she was wondering that herself. But he didn't.

Then she heard scuffling and footsteps behind them, and she didn't have to wonder anymore.

Someone was chasing them.

She tried to move faster, and hoped Drew could keep up. Finally, she got to the access conduit and shoved it open. When Drew came through, they slammed it closed. Emiko threw the latch into place, then activated a hazard seal.

A red light went on overhead, and a low keening noise began.

Drew must have known what a hazard seal was, because he said, "It'll take two minutes for all the conduits to close. They could still get in from another point."

She was impressed, but she'd tell him that later. Instead, they ran. Fortunately, a red light had activated along the footpath, showing them the quickest way out. Emiko was grateful for that, because the labyrinthine, winding tunnels would have been easy to mistake for one another in their haste.

Finally, they came to a steep flight of stairs. "That ought to take us up to the main tram complex."

They rushed up the stairs, only to have their path blocked by two people clad in black from neck to toe.

Scrap.

They couldn't go back, and they couldn't get past these two. They'd have to fight.

Emiko didn't wait. She rushed in fast, shoving one against the other, then throwing a punch.

The man absorbed the shove and dodged the punch, and she knew they weren't up against amateurs. This was the real thing.

Fight smarter. Be stronger. She took up a relative position to Drew, to take the pair on one-on-one while keeping him in her sightline.

She let a punch glance off her shoulder so she could slip in under his guard and deliver a strike to the temple. She followed that up with a palm strike to his sternum, and then a right cross. She connected well with the first two, but he blocked the last.

They threw blow after blow at one another, but neither of them gained the upper hand. They were too evenly matched.

She'd have to go with a different plan.

Using both palms against his sternum, she knocked him back slightly, then kicked his knee. With her right leg forward, she grabbed a small knife she'd secured against her inner thigh.

It was in her fingers only for a microsecond, it seemed. Her body followed her motion, snapping the knife forward. It embedded itself into the guy's chest, directly over his heart. He fell over backward and lay still.

She turned to Drew and the man he was still fighting.

"Enough." A voice behind them said.

The remaining assailant stepped back, palms facing outward, and made a small bow. Warily, Drew backed away from him before looking toward the voice.

From the shadows, a PAC admiral stepped out. Emiko didn't know him, which seemed impossible since she'd memorized the names and faces of all admirals currently serving the PAC. But the bars on his uniform indicated he was indeed an admiral.

Still, Emiko still didn't relax her guard. She trusted only Drew until she knew what was going on.

"At ease, Cadet Arashi. That's an order." The admiral stared her down.

She wasn't a cadet yet, not until she was accepted into OTS. But she adjusted her stance and held her arms behind her back as a cadet would.

"Report. Debrief me on your mission," the admiral ordered.

"Regret that I cannot, sir. I do not have permission to speak about my orders." She returned his gaze, unblinking. She could relay nothing without Martinez's authorization, regardless of the admiral's rank. Clandestine operations went beyond the typical chain of command.

Sometimes it went beyond justice, too. People could do bad things for good reasons. And sometimes, agents got burned for nothing but being caught up in a bad situation.

Was this one of those cases?

"You, then." He nodded to Drew. "Debrief me or you'll end up in the brig like this one."

"I regret that I cannot, sir." Drew stood in the same stance she did.

"Then I have no choice but to remand you to the proper authorities. I hope you're prepared for what's to come."

Drew said nothing, nor did she.

The admiral paused, then, amazingly, smiled. "Congratulations. You two are officially accepted into OTS, and the clandestine operations division of intelligence. I'm Admiral Krazinski, and I will be your sole commanding officer from this point forward."

Whelkin stepped out of the shadows to join them, smiling.

Then the dead man on the ground sat up.

"All of this was fake?" Drew asked.

"Not fake," Whelkin said. "The people at the academy branch office had no idea what was going on. That was a legit infiltration. We did set up the situation on the tram, though."

"And the fight was real," Krazinski added. "We just took some precautions to keep you from killing some of your fellow operatives."

"Seems wise," Drew said.

Emiko eyed him to see if he was cracking a joke, but it was hard to tell with him.

"I don't have to tell you to say nothing to anyone about any of this," the admiral said. "Continue back to Earth, as planned. Continue your classes. Soon, you will get your team assignments and begin training with them. We'll be in touch." The admiral gave them a shallow bow.

Drew immediately bowed more deeply in response, and Emiko quickly did the same.

She found all this strange. "That's it?"

She shouldn't talk out of turn like that with an admiral, but she hadn't expected her acceptance into the program to come inside a grungy tram system, while wearing a short skirt and, undoubtedly, giving her underwear a liberal showing-around.

It was anti-climactic. But maybe she'd have to get used to things unfolding in unexpected ways from now on.

"Oh no, Emiko," the admiral assured her before turning away. "This is just the beginning. I hope you're ready."

She hoped so, too.

The voyage back to Earth felt like a victory lap to Emiko. She and Drew took a four-hour nap before taking off from the docking station to ensure alertness, but it had taken her an hour just to fall asleep.

"You okay?" Drew asked once they'd gotten underway. "You've been quiet."

"Just watching everything. I keep expecting some ships to come out and attack us."

"I wondered about that, too. I've been watching for any odd communication activity. Think they'd spring another test on us so quickly?"

She shrugged. "If they wanted to, yes. Why not pile on us, and see how hard they can push us before we break?"

"Makes sense. I guess we'll see."

"I kind of hope they do attack us. I'd like a chance to try combat maneuvers for real." But try as she might, she found no trace of suspicious activity.

"I didn't know you were such a daredevil." Drew regarded her with a speculative expression.

"Neither did I, before I got to the academy. But apparently I am."

"I like that you're fearless. It's sexy." He grinned at her.

She chuckled. "I'm definitely not fearless. It's just that, in an extreme situation, fear doesn't matter. It's useless, so it gets shoved to the bottom, below all the feelings, senses, and skills that are useful."

"I know what you mean. Some people panic under pressure

and some people only get sharper. I don't think it's something you can do anything about. It's just instinctive reflex."

She liked that. "Is that a personal theory or have you done some research on that?"

"Personal theory. But now that you've questioned me, I feel honor bound to follow up with some research."

"Do that, and get back to me." After a beat, she added, "I think you're right. I've always been at my best during tense situations. And the higher the stakes get, the more alive I feel."

"Yep. I've already diagnosed you as an adrenaline junkie. Classic case." He shot her a taunting look.

"You liked it as much as I did," she pretended to grumble. "Admit it. When those guys appeared at the top of those stairs, you were itching to fight."

"Maybe not as much as you. But yeah. I was ready," he admitted.

"We need to work on your technique, though. Next time, I want you to take your guy down, then come help me with mine."

"What? Why should I do more than my fair share?"

"I dunno. You're bigger. I guess." She grinned at him. "It would just be nice for me to have options, you know."

"I'll work on it."

She liked how they could talk about something serious, and she could tell him he needed to up his game, while keeping the mood relaxed and easy. He'd held his own against that operative, but she'd seen that he was outmatched.

She hoped that once she got assigned to a team, her teammates would have the same ability to communicate frankly without egos getting in the way.

The assault she was hoping for never came, so her next challenge was her first real atmospheric landing. Most ships docked at the orbital docking station above a planet, leaving people to come down in the elevator. That meant she would do such a landing only on very rare occasions.

She intended to do it perfectly.

She double-checked all of her readings, then double-checked her coordinates and variables.

"Time to get the straps on," she advised Drew as she secured her own straps. "This will feel kind of intense."

"Great. I'll just sit here while you do all the work."

"The computer will do a lot of it. We'll be dropping like a bag of cement through the atmosphere until I have enough lift to be able to manually control us. We'll execute some turns to burn off excess energy, and then I'll fly us in."

He put his headset on. "You make it sound so fun."

His tone indicated that it did not sound like fun to him.

She said, "Yeah," with great enthusiasm.

The real thing felt exactly like the simulator. The only difference was knowing that she was *actually* plummeting in a little ship toward the Earth's surface at a relative free fall of epic proportions.

Then she got down to around six thousand meters from the surface and took control, getting a feel for this ship and then flying it down to the surface for a landing not unlike a large aircraft.

When they finally rolled to a stop, she looked to Drew. He wore an alert, curious expression.

"Well, now we've done that," he said matter-of-factly. "Let's go see what comes next."

AFTER THEIR MISSION TOGETHER, a chasm that had stood between Emiko and Drew closed. They could now talk openly with each other about their training, intentions, and prospects. Everything they'd left unsaid before, they could now discuss.

They took careful precautions to avoid being overheard. It became second nature for them to sweep her room for listening devices and remain aware of people who might be in their proximity. She felt freed, though, to finally be able to talk to someone about her hopes, concerns, and suspicions.

The closer she felt to him, the more she wondered about her team assignment. She didn't get nervous about much, but after feeling so aligned with Drew during their academy experience, she wondered if it would be possible to have such an intuitive relationship with others during her OTS years.

She needed to brace herself for a harsh change. She resolved to savor the time she had left with Drew, but prepare for their relationship to come to a necessary end. They had only five months until graduation, and who knew where their differing specialties would lead them?

If it happened that way, the short stream of days ahead would compose the tail end of their relationship.

She intended to enjoy the time as much as she could, outside of her studies. Her classes remained rigorous, but in the two weeks after their Luna mission, her other training had waned. Whelkin summoned her less, and her flight training had lessened a great deal.

What did it mean?

She was curled up on her bed with an infoboard one evening while Drew sat at the voicecom doing who-knows-what to some computer network. It was their usual evening routine.

Her comport beeped, and his did the same almost instantaneously.

They shared a look before seeing to whatever had come their way.

Come to the administrative building, room two seventy-five, immediately. Krazinski.

"Two seventy-five?" Drew asked.

"Yep. Let's go."

"Should we, like, do anything first?" he wondered.

"Like what?"

"I don't know. I feel like we should dress up or wash our hands or something."

She snorted and knocked into him on her way to the door. "Let's go."

Emiko and Drew made it to the room within minutes, but in spite of their haste, they had not been the first ones to arrive.

She immediately recognized the two other students sitting to the right of the door. It would be hard not to. The guy was a tank. He looked right about her age, but looked to be over two meters tall and probably even heavier than he looked. He had dark hair, tanned skin, and a rough-around-the-edges look that made him stand out at the PAC Academy as much as his size did. She had shared no classes with him, though, or exchanged any words with him.

The woman was big, too, but obviously a human from Zerellus. The colony included many people with dark blonde hair and tanned skin. Her height and muscular build were unusual.

Emiko wished she could put on that kind of muscle.

She noticed that they had taken the seats furthest from the door, leaving her and Drew no choice but to sit on the seats more exposed to the doorway.

It made her feel edgy.

"Good," Krazinski said. "Now that we're all here, I'll get right to it. I have personally selected the four of you to be on a black-op team that I will run. I will be your sole commanding officer, though you will be expected to follow orders from other ranking officers as you would for someone befitting your rank. Exceptions apply, of course, in terms of classified information."

Emiko wasn't sure what to process first. On one hand, she was beyond elated to realize that she and Drew would be on the same team. Though Whelkin had said they were looking for a team of four, she hadn't dared to hope that she and Drew would both make it, and both be placed on that team.

It meant that they could continue their relationship and the openness they'd only recently developed.

However, the two people on the other side of the room were not what she'd expected. They looked rough. More like mercenaries than officers. Would she be able to rely on them like she could on Drew?

She looked at their hard expressions and their standoffish postures and doubted it.

"Here are your covert identities. Study yours. Study those of your team. Learn to work together. If you make it through OTS, you graduate as a team. If you wash out, you wash out as a team. From this moment onward, there is no one more important in your lives than the people in this room. Myself included."

After giving them all a long, hard look, he handed an infoboard to each.

Drew spoke first, which didn't surprise her. "Avian unit. I'm Raptor."

"Hawk," the big bear of a guy said, his voice deep and gruff.

"Peregrine," the woman said.

Emiko frowned at her infoboard. "This says…Fallon."

"That's Falcon," Krazinski said.

"No, it says Fallon." She hated correcting an admiral, but no amount of obedience could make an *l* into a *c*.

She handed it to Krazinski, and, after a moment, he huffed out an annoyed breath. "A clerical error. Inexcusable. I'll get it corrected."

It felt like an inauspicious beginning, to her. If she were one to buy into bad luck harbingers, this would probably count as one.

The admiral continued, "The four of you will begin training together soon. In the meantime, I recommend you spend as much time together as possible, getting to understand one another. Additional details will be provided when you need them. So, for now, I'll bid you goodnight and leave you to get acquainted."

He paused at the door. "Congratulations on getting this far. But I'm going to expect a great deal of you four, individually and as a team."

Then he was gone, leaving her and Drew eyeing the other two.

They looked no more enthusiastic.

She started things off. "My name on campus is Emiko. My cover is a security officer. My specialties are piloting and combat."

She saw instant disdain on their faces. They didn't think she could fight.

Tamping down on her irritation at their disrespect, she looked to Drew.

"My campus name is Drew. I guess you'll know me as Raptor. I quite like that name, I have to say. My specialties are hacking and system infiltration."

"Aren't those the same thing?" Peregrine asked.

"Similar. But not the same." Drew answered with an easy grin, but it didn't melt her icy demeanor.

"My name here is Poppy. It's a stupid name. Peregrine is better. I specialize in small electronics and disguises."

"Disguises?" Drew perked up. "Like, makeup and wigs and stuff?"

"It's a lot more than that. It's prosthetics, understanding and being able to reproduce accents, and changing your body language and the way you move. Complete immersion into another character."

Her reproachful tone didn't faze him. "Cool. I look forward to learning from you."

That made her look more closely at him, and while her expression didn't warm up, it didn't look so glacial, either.

The tank glared at them. "Olag on campus. Hawk to you, I

guess. I specialize in getting shit done." His eyes narrowed, as if daring them to say something about his lack of specificity.

Drew grinned. "Awesome. I love getting shit done."

Emiko remembered what Whelkin had said about being recruited as a leader. That meant she would have to lead these three very large personalities. Right now, that meant deferring to Drew to handle these early moments, because he was better with people than she was. If anyone could build a bridge to the two brutes on the other side of the room, it was him.

An important part of leading was letting others do what they did best.

Hawk frowned at Drew, but it was more a look of consideration than disapproval.

"Do you two know each other already?" Drew asked them.

"We've had some classes together," Hawk said. "You two?"

"Yeah," Drew said. "We met during our first year and have gotten to know each other well."

"Right. Is there anything else we're supposed to do here?" Hawk glanced around at the other three.

Emiko sensed that he'd had enough of being cooped up with them under these circumstances. "No, I think we can all go whenever we want. We'll meet up again soon enough."

She kept her tone unthreatening and straightforward, but not so soft as to be perceived as weak.

Hawk stood. "Good. Until whenever that happens."

Then he was gone.

Emiko had expected Peregrine to follow in his wake, but she remained, eyeing them.

"He and I aren't together," she stated flatly. "We just know each other."

A horribly awkward silence fell. Emiko wished Drew would say something to smooth things over, but he didn't.

"Well, I look forward to getting to know you, too," she finally said. "Is Hawk always this abrupt?"

"Generally. He had to fight to get here, and he fights every day to stay here. I think fighting is natural to him."

Finally, Emiko felt they might have something in common. "Same here."

Peregrine remained blank faced. Emiko decided this would be her role model in learning to do that, because Peregrine had it down cold.

"I guess we'll see," Peregrine answered. "Anything else you want to say here?"

Emiko felt like this was her moment to say something inspirational that would pull them together as a team. She didn't come up with anything. "I've worked hard in an effort to be the best. That's not going to stop. But now, I'll work hard for all you three, too, to make sure we're the best team."

Peregrine flipped her long blond ponytail back over her shoulder. "I guess that's a start."

6

Emiko struggled to keep an even expression. As the team leader, it was her responsibility to see that she and Raptor got to know Hawk and Peregrine.

They weren't making it easy. Hawk refused any purely social situations. Asking him to dinner or have a drink or two failed every time. Since they hadn't been given any specific training exercises together, that left Emiko at a loss. She kept trying, though. She even visited his room to try to glean a little information about him. Maybe being in his space would get him to let his guard down just a little.

She stood in the doorway to his room. From what she could see, although he was in a building on the other side of campus, his room was similar to hers, as if they'd been stamped out of the same cookie cutter.

"What about your studies?" she persisted after he turned her down again to join her for a meal. "Is there anything you could use a study partner for?"

He frowned at her, but his gaze dropped to the floor and his body swayed slightly. Aha. She had him.

"Final grades matter, you know. I heard of a guy who washed

out even after getting an assignment because he failed one of his classes."

She'd heard no such thing, but she said it with authority.

One side of his nose wrinkled, like a dog thinking about snapping at its handler.

"Which one's giving you trouble?" she pressed.

"Math," he growled, sounding as if the admission wasn't easy for him. "Never been my strong suit."

She didn't smile. She sensed it would be the wrong approach for him. Instead, she maintained a no-nonsense expression. "As it happens, I'm damn good at it. Let's get to work."

He hesitated, and she felt a thrill of victory.

"I've got stuff going on today." He'd returned to his gruff, forceful tone. "We can meet tomorrow evening. Dinner's on you, *Fallon,* and don't be skimpy." He emphasized the use of her misprinted name.

The door closed in her face. If it weren't mechanical, she was pretty sure he would have slammed it.

No matter. She'd made inroads with him, and that was what counted. Maybe she was cut out to be the team leader, after all.

Next, she had to figure out how to reach out to Peregrine.

Again, Emiko found herself outside the door of her team member. Instead of being hostile, though, Peregrine looked bored. Inconvenienced.

"I don't do study groups. Sorry." When she moved to close the door, Emiko edged in, causing the mechanism to abort.

"Don't come for the studying, then. But the rest of us will be there. Do you really want to be the only one not making an effort to be part of the team? I mean, it's early. I don't know how permanent these assignments are if there's one person not making an effort."

Peregrine's chin came up, and she looked down at Emiko. Her expression remained blank.

Emiko really wanted to learn how to do that.

"Fine. I'll come."

"Great. I'm bringing Bennite food. Stew and bread are my favorite, but is there something you'd prefer?"

Peregrine frowned. "No. I love their stew and bread. Just make sure you get lots."

This time, Emiko smiled. She had a gut sense it was the right thing to do. "I keep hearing that. I'll bring plenty."

Emiko called in the food order to the Bennite place and paid extra to have it delivered. She didn't want to carry enough takeout for fifteen people by herself. The cost had been significant, and she was far from rich, but she considered it an investment in her career.

She needed this study session to go well.

They couldn't meet in the library because of the food, and none of them had a dorm room big enough to be comfortable for four. She didn't want to meet on the quad, either, because it felt indiscreet.

Instead, she'd taken time to set up the basement training room she used with Whelkin. She'd set up two folding tables and chairs, and tossed some blankets and pillows on the floor.

She had Jane and Val to thank for the blankets and pillows. They hadn't even asked why she needed them. She owed them one. She'd miss them after graduation. Though she had almost nothing in common with them, they'd proven to be good friends over these past three years.

She met the delivery guy at the lift, and gave him a nice tip. Then she took the food down the hall to the room and arranged it on a table.

It smelled amazing. She fought the urge to dig in, and waited.

Drew was the first to arrive. No, she needed to think of him as Raptor now. She used the name Drew in front of others, but tried to remember to think of him as Raptor.

"Where are the others?" he asked, coming close to the food and taking a deep breath. "Mmm. Do we have to wait for them?"

"Dig in. I get the feeling they'd find it weird if we waited. I don't think they care for formalities like that, but I felt odd starting on my own."

He wasted no time grabbing a bowl of stew and a spoon. "Good thinking."

"Plus, it means you can eat now, instead of later, right?" she laughed.

"Absolutely," he said around a mouthful of stew.

"How did your practicals go today?" She sat in a chair and pulled a bowl of stew toward her.

"Good. I'll be glad when they're done, though. I feel like my brain is fried with all the memorizing I've had to do. It's not practical. No one memorizes everything. You keep sheets of things you need."

She carefully peeled the lid off her stew. Steam rolled out and condensation dripped off the top into her food. "It's not about the things you're memorizing. It's about pushing you to the breaking point, and seeing how you do under pressure. It's about finding the best."

He nodded, his mouth too full to speak.

Hawk came through the door, instantly making the room feel much more populated. "Is this where you two train with Whelkin?"

She and Raptor exchanged a look.

"What?" Hawk said. "That can't be a secret anymore."

He had a point.

Emiko pushed a bowl of soup toward him. "Help yourself."

Hawk picked up a chair and set it down further away from

her. The chair wasn't heavy, but he handled it like it had no weight.

She wanted to keep him talking, since he seemed inclined to. "Why do you think Whelkin hasn't put us together to train?"

Hawk wiped his mouth with a napkin. "Easy. The class championships are coming up and he doesn't want us learning each other's styles. The top brass wants to see how we approach each other as unknown quantities."

Huh. That made perfect sense. What other clever insights might Hawk have?

Peregrine entered silently, picked up some food, then sat on the floor against the wall. She gave them a nod, but said nothing.

Emiko sighed inwardly. These two weren't going to make this easy.

She looked to Raptor. He was the charming one.

Raptor hitched his shoulders up in a shrug. Some help he was.

Right. It was up to her. What could the four of them possibly have in common? They needed some interest or topic of conversation to break the ice.

She didn't come up with anything.

They continued eating, and as she chewed a piece of bread, she decided to try asking them about their specialties. If they didn't share any interests, then she could show interest in their talents.

"Peregrine, you said you're into small electronics, is that right?"

Peregrine looked up, swallowed, and said, "Yes."

Emiko waited for more, but no such luck. "Repairing or creating?"

"Both. Anything. I used to do more modding of existing hardware, but since I got here, I've been doing more creating from scratch."

Yes! Emiko had gotten an entire sentence out of her! Plus, it had yielded actual information.

Hawk turned to look at her, looking interested. "Modding as in typical stuff or as in illegal mods."

Peregrine looked at him a long moment, as if weighing her answer. "Mostly illegal. At least, those were the fun ones."

Hawk smiled. "Nice."

"Why is that nice?" Peregrine asked.

"A lot of what I'm good at leans toward the not-legal side, as well." He bit off a huge hunk of bread and chewed.

"Really?" Peregrine sat straighter. "Like what?"

He returned his attention to his stew. "This and that."

Emiko thought he'd retreated back into himself again, but then he added, "I'm good at navigating dangerous places and dealing with dangerous people."

He looked up at her. "How about you, Fallon?"

Drew—no, Raptor—chuckled at the use of her misprinted name, and it made her smile, too. Maybe Hawk would turn out to be funny, if he ever let his guard down.

"What about me?" she asked. "I already told you my specialties. Flying and fighting."

"Flying what? Fighting how?"

"I'll fly anything. If someone put wings on a clothes processor, I'd fly it. I can fly drones, too. Same thing for fighting. Hand-to-hand, weapons, anything." She shrugged.

"She's a heck of a knife thrower," Raptor offered.

Hawk gave him a long, hard look. "How long have you two been a couple?"

Raptor blinked, but recovered quickly. "Since about halfway through the first year. Is that problematic for you?"

"Not unless you make it a problem, with fighting or whatever. Just keep your personal shit clear of our work."

"Not a problem," Raptor answered breezily. "I make it a point to keep all personal shit out of my work."

Emiko wanted to see Hawk smile at that, but he didn't.

The energy went out of the room and she felt disappointed. For a second there, she thought they'd been getting somewhere.

Hawk crushed his bowl in his hands and shoved it into one of the bags the food had come in. "Should we get the math stuff over with? I have plans tonight, so I only have two hours left."

Emiko had to fight a frown. She tried to embody Peregrine's steely expression. She was annoyed, though. What plans could he have that were more important than making sure his grades were where they needed to be?

How had this guy even made it into the academy?

"Let's get to work," she said.

Two hours later, Fallon thought it was safe to say that all four of them were tense. Hawk did not suffer math well, and Peregrine's sullen silence had made Fallon feel like she was being judged.

At least Hawk had made a little progress in his ability to work through the equations. That progress had been hard earned, as the rest of them had to suffer frequent outbursts like, "Why do I even need to know this? I'll never use this!"

Now, he said, "Time's up. I'm outta here."

Just like that, he strutted out.

Peregrine gathered the trash. "I'll take these to the recycler." At the door, she paused. "Thanks for the help. Math isn't my favorite, either."

Once they were alone, Raptor rubbed Fallon's shoulders.

"It could have been worse, right?" she asked, leaning back against him.

"Much worse," he agreed. "Much, much worse. We should be cautiously optimistic."

She let out the sigh she felt like she'd been holding for hours.

"I hope you're right."

THE NEXT TIME she did one-on-one training with Whelkin, she took the opportunity to talk to him about her team.

"Raptor and I make sense as teammates. Peregrine and Hawk are very different than us." She sat, sweaty and rumpled, on the floor of the training room.

Whelkin looked sympathetic. "Teams are put together very carefully based on the skills each member has. You four were selected because your combined areas of expertise will make you highly effective."

"Is any consideration put into personalities?"

"Personality is irrelevant. It's up to you four to figure out how to work together. A lot of that burden falls on you as the team leader."

"Do they know about that bit yet?" she asked.

"Raptor does. Not the others."

"I'm sure that will be a great conversation," she said sourly. "Hawk has a temper. Maybe Peregrine does, too. It's hard to tell what she's thinking."

"There's a lot more to Hawk than it seems. Keep working at it. Peregrine's even harder to know. It will take time."

"Do you have a team?" she asked, suddenly curious about his experiences.

"Yes. Two of them, in fact."

"Two? How?"

He took so long to answer that she thought he would tell her it was classified information and he could divulge nothing.

But he finally said, "My first team got ambushed. It was a hostile planet, and all three of them died. I nearly did, too. A year later, I was assigned to another team. We lost one member after three years, to a sniper. A year later, we lost another on an undercover mission. And the third never got over the death of the first one. He would have, eventually, but he got reckless. He made a mistake. And then there was just me again."

"I'm sorry." It seemed like a woefully inadequate thing to say about losing six teammates.

One side of his mouth turned down in a wry expression. "I had worse luck than most, but few teams make it five years together without losing a member. The career you're aiming for doesn't give you great odds of living to see old age."

"I know." She'd always known that. Having someone who had seen operatives die, though, made the danger feel closer.

"Do you? When you're nineteen, dying gloriously sounds like a great idea. Right up until you get knifed in the belly and lie in an alley watching your blood pour out of you while you're unable to do anything about it. I promise you, when that happens, it will not feel glorious. It will feel shitty and stupid and pointless. You'll die alone and scared, like everyone else." He suddenly looked much older. Maybe it was the sadness, or the knowing, in his eyes.

"Yeah," she said softly. "I know that."

"Good."

"Do you say this to all your students?" she asked.

"Yes."

"Are you hoping they'll drop out?"

He shook his head slightly. "Yes and no. I hate getting to know such bright, talented young people, and knowing that their futures are bound to be ugly. But then, someone has to do this job, and only the best can."

"So why give the speech?"

"So that when I get your fatality report, I know that I warned you, and that you made an informed choice."

"Wow." She stared at him, trying to imagine how it would feel to hear about the death of someone she'd trained.

"Yep. You and I live in a world of hard realities."

"Someone has to," she pointed out. "So that the general public doesn't have to know about those realities."

He smiled sadly. "Recognizing that is why you're the team leader. You've got that hero gene that enables a person to put her ship on a suicide course, if that's what needs to happen. You have the ability to see clearly and make the right choices under pressure."

"Hero gene," she repeated.

"There's probably a better word for it. But it would amount to the same thing. That's how I know you'll figure out how to make Avian unit into a real team."

"Were you the leader of your teams?" she asked.

"Yes."

"How did you unite them?"

His sad smile returned. "Doesn't matter. Your team is different. Only you can find what will work for you four."

"Right."

She was on her own.

THE DAY after Emiko's talk with Whelkin, she went on her first stealth mission.

Never mind that it was self-assigned rather than a mandate from her superiors. She had a mission and a goal.

She'd make friends with Hawk if it killed her. The way she figured it, if she didn't, their lack of camaraderie would end up killing them anyway.

Was it too soon? Was she pushing too hard? There was something to be said for an organic approach and letting things develop in their own time.

Then she remembered Whelkin's words. She wasn't going to lose her team. She'd use brute force now to prevent losing them later.

Raptor had patched into security feeds so she could track Hawk's movements the night before. She couldn't risk tailing him right from his dorm, because he'd surely notice her at some point.

Instead, she put herself in his path in the downtown area of the adjacent city. As she waited inside a store across the street, looking out the window to the tram drop-off site, she hoped Hawk was a creature of habit. Or at the least, his recent favorite routine would prove to be consistent.

Success.

As the tram moved away, she saw an unmistakable large figure receding into the distance, toward the bar he'd visited the night before.

Yes!

She counted out two minutes, pretending to admire some clothing, then proceeded to acquire her target.

She went through an old-fashioned wooden door with a huge metal handle, then quickly assessed the bar. A wide, open space with lots of small tables and chairs scattered around. Not too many at this early hour. Aside from the entrance she'd just come through, she noted two additional exits.

Hawk's back was to her as he sat on one of the stools that lined the edge of the long, dark surface of the bar.

She sat on the stool next to him, telling the bartender, "I'll have what he's having."

She'd always wanted to say that.

Hawk gave her a long look. "Not sure you can handle it." He tapped his tall mug. "This has a lot of kick."

"You'd be surprised what I can handle." She held his gaze, unblinking.

She could have asked Jane or Val for an injection to counteract the effects of alcohol, but that would have felt like cheating. If she was going to do this, she had to do it right. She had, however, eaten a full meal beforehand.

She didn't think of it as cheating. Just tactical thinking.

"Whatever." He shrugged. "Just don't expect me to carry you home."

"Back at you. I'm stronger than I look, but I'm not moving you anywhere without a complex set of pulleys."

He smirked.

Score! At least he seemed to have a sense of humor hidden under there somewhere. She felt mildly encouraged.

Her drink arrived and she took a careful sip.

Her burning sinuses alerted her to the fact that this was not the way to get this particular beverage down.

She blew out a long breath, then held it, taking several fast gulps, then turned her head to blow out another long breath. She hoped Hawk didn't notice.

He did. He all-out smirked at her this time.

"Okay," she admitted, "it's higher-octane than I tend to drink. But it's fine."

He drained his mug in response, taking the glass from three-quarters full all the way down.

Prelin's ass. Her work was cut out for her.

The bartender returned, shoving a basket of pretzel knots at Hawk. They looked good, all brown on top and speckled with salt. Then the smell hit her, making them even more appealing.

She considered before acting. Hawk seemed to be the kind of guy who was always on the offensive. She guessed—hoped—that brazen behavior was the way to go with him.

This thought process took only a moment. Within a moment of the bartender bringing it, she snatched a pretzel knot out of the basket.

Hawk squinted at her, then grabbed one for himself. "These things are awesome."

She bit in, and the chewy outside and the moist inside, combined with the saltiness, made her sigh with pleasure.

"Yep," Hawk said.

He was being surprisingly agreeable. She'd half-expected him to roar at her until she left his watering hole.

Actually, more than half.

She chugged back a few more gulps of the drink. She didn't even know what it was called. It could have lighter fluid in it, for all she knew.

No matter. She was on a mission.

Every time he took a drink, she drank. Every time he ate a pretzel, she grabbed another. She sat next to him, saying nothing.

After he drained another mug and punched an order into his menuboard for another, he sighed.

"What do you want, skinny girl?"

She refused to be baited. "I want to get to know you."

"Why?"

"It's my job."

His head went to the left so slowly that it didn't look like a shake of the head, but then it proceeded to the right side, too. "Rich girl like you, from a military family, has nothing in common with me. Don't bother."

She allowed a smile to curl up one side of her mouth so he could see it. "You checked up on me. Good. I like people who are thorough."

He scowled at her.

"But I'm far from rich. We lived a very modest lifestyle in a very expensive place. Yes, I had certain privileges. That doesn't mean I didn't fight to get where I am."

She hoped that would lead him into revealing more about his background, but he just stared at her thoughtfully.

He wasn't dumb. The awareness came to her in a flash. She saw cunning in his eyes. Calculation. Math might not be his thing, but he knew people. He could figure them out by watching them.

This was why he was on her team. That was how he fit.

She smiled.

"What's funny?" he asked. "I want to laugh, too."

She looked at him from the corner of her eye. "I'm not laughing. I just realized why we were teamed up."

"Yeah? Why?"

"Because you can go places I can't, and can understand people in a different way than I do."

The aggressive set of his shoulders eased. "Good. As long as you know you're not better than me, this might actually work."

She grinned. "Oh, I am better. I fully intend to win all the championships for our class."

He looked annoyed, but the expression quickly morphed into wry amusement. Yet he said nothing.

Neither did she. Instead, she drained her mug of Pure Hell, as she'd privately named the beverage, following it up by blowing out a long breath to get rid of the lingering vapor burn.

"You drink well, *Fallon,*" Hawk said, putting stress on the name. "That's something, at least."

She didn't respond, other than a shrug. He wasn't ready to share anything with her, or ask anything about herself. But she'd gone toe to toe with him and showed that she was worth considering, at the least.

For tonight, it was enough.

ALTHOUGH EMIKO HAD EATEN as many pretzels as she could, while sticking Hawk with the bill for them, by the time she returned to her dorm, she felt light-headed. Light in general, actually.

Raptor looked up as she entered. "How'd it go?"

"Better than expected." She made an *okay* symbol with her fingers. "Still work to do, but mission accomplished."

His forehead crinkled. "Have you been drinking?"

"A little. Why?"

"You seem a little...drunk."

She frowned. "That's probably why the bed's slanted."

He chuckled. "Yep. That'll do it. What happened?"

She closed the gap between her and the bed. Funny. On the tram, she hadn't felt so hazy. "Did my job. He's clever. Doesn't trust people."

He stood, and she knew he intended to help her to the bed. She wanted to do it herself, so she hurried. She flopped onto the bed.

"I'll get you some water." He left, presumably going to the common area to get chilled water.

She watched his butt as he went. He had a cute one.

When he returned, carrying a bottle of water, she giggled.

"What?" he asked.

"I like your butt." She accepted the water and drank, knowing that if she didn't, she'd have a nasty headache the next day.

He took the compliment in stride. "Good to know."

She pushed the mostly empty bottle back into his hands. "I'm tired."

"I bet. It's late."

She flopped over sideways, a little harder than she intended. With her head on the pillow, she wriggled to push the sheet and blanket down, then back up over her.

"I guess that's goodnight, then," he said, helping her with the covers.

Her eyes popped open. "He called me Fallon again. I think he might be kind of funny."

"Interesting." He patted her head and got up from the bed.

She knew he was patronizing her, but was too tired to care. She rarely stayed up so late, much less drank so much.

"I have to start working on Peregrine next," she yawned. She meant to say more, because thoughts were unspooling in her mind, as they always did, but she gave in to the haze of sleep calling to her.

7

Emiko woke up with a headache. She refused to do anything about it but let time sort things out. She rarely did such destructive things to her body, but since she had, she deserved to live with the results.

A lingering headache made for a rough day in class, though, and by the time she got to the end of the day, she was grateful to flop onto her bed and close her eyes. Raptor was still gone, and as much as she enjoyed his company, having a little bit of quiet time meant everything at that moment.

She woke to the smell of Bennite stew. Was she dreaming it? She hadn't even realized she'd fallen asleep.

"I thought that would bring you around." Raptor sat next to her with the heavenly smelling bag of food.

"No words," she said. "Just food."

He laughed, putting a bowl of stew into her hands, then sticking a spoon in. "This ought to fix you up. I don't know how the Bennites put healing properties into their food, but this stuff is not only delicious, it's great for hangovers."

"I wouldn't know." Though she felt cranky, she was glad to shovel the thick, meaty stew into her mouth.

"Right," he said. "I bet hangovers are too undisciplined for you."

"Something like that." She talked with her mouth full. She didn't care.

"It's good to see you being pushed out of your comfort zone."

She stopped eating to frown at him. "I don't have a comfort zone."

"Sure you do. You like things that can be summed up, diagnosed, and solved. You don't like things that make you deal with messy psychological stuff."

"I'm dealing. I already dealt. And I'll deal some more. With Hawk, and with Peregrine next. I need to work at figuring her out."

He handed her a napkin. She took that as a not very subtle hint to wipe her mouth.

He said, "What if there's no figuring either of them out? Maybe it's more about accepting them."

Her minor irritation stopped being minor. "If you have something to say, just lay it out."

"I'm just saying that they seem to be from a background very different from yours. Not that I'm making assumptions about your first life, or theirs. Sometimes there's no middle ground. Maybe you shouldn't push too hard. Not everything can be forced."

She stopped eating. "You think I'm going about this wrong?"

"I think you should consider the possibility."

She did, for about thirty seconds. Then she stood, putting the food aside. "No. I already thought this through, and I talked to Whelkin for his experience. You and I have been trained for different functions. You can't assume that you know more about my job than I do."

She grabbed a water bottle. "I'm going for a walk."

She left the room without looking back at him.

Taking a walk cleared Emiko's head, but didn't resolve her irritation with Raptor.

No, it wasn't irritation, exactly. It was disappointment. Realization. Yes, that was it. Until now, she'd never felt the burden of command that would fall on her, in terms of her relationship with him.

She'd have to make decisions that he might not understand. He might not agree with them, either. That happened in military situations. But would their personal relationship affect his ability to take commands from her and respect her choices?

Even worse, would her relationship with him affect her judgment?

She'd been thrilled to learn that her relationship with him wouldn't have to end when they entered OTS. That they'd both be working in clandestine ops and could talk about their lives.

Maybe she'd been wrong. Maybe they couldn't be both teammates and lovers.

She walked along the perimeter of the campus. The night air was clear and pleasant. Bugs in the distance created a soothing chorus of chirping and buzzing.

On she walked until her feet felt sore. Then she found herself in front of Peregrine's door. Unplanned and entirely uninvited.

She touched the chime anyway.

If Peregrine was surprised to see her, she covered it well.

"How do you do that?" Emiko asked.

"Do what?"

"Not let your feelings show."

"Natural tendency. Most people find it bothersome."

"Not me," Emiko assured her. "I've been working on it, but I'm still not good enough yet."

Peregrine stared at her for a long moment. "Did you want to come in?"

Emiko hadn't dared to hope for such an invitation, but she didn't show her excitement. "Sure. Thanks."

"Do you want some tea or something?" Peregrine asked as Emiko pulled the chair away from the desk and sat on it. The only other option was the bed, and she didn't know Peregrine well enough to sit on her bed.

"No, but thank you for offering."

Peregrine sat on her bed. "So why are you here?"

"I'm not sure. I was walking around campus, thinking about the team, and I ended up here. I don't know anything about you, and I'd like to change that."

"There's not a lot to know about me," Peregrine said. "I haven't done much. Haven't seen much. You already know I like electronics and disguises."

Peregrine shrugged. She seemed forthcoming enough, but apparently found nothing about herself worth talking about.

Did she have a self-confidence issue?

Emiko latched onto the last thing she said. "How did you get into disguises? That doesn't seem like something that a person's commonly exposed to."

Peregrine ran her hand down her ponytail, which hung down her front, and tossed it back over her shoulder. Emiko had noticed her do that before. It seemed to be a habit.

"I needed some elective classes, so I signed up for art my first term. I figured it would be an easy grade, since art is subjective."

"Was it?"

Peregrine shook her head. "Hardly. We did brief modules on things like painting and sculpting, but they were a basis for doing digital and 3D art. I teamed up with another student to do a project. He created a 3D rendered bust of an ancient Greek god, and my job was to paint it and finish it with hair and whatnot to make it lifelike. That's when it clicked with me. Creating realistic skin tones and lifelike textures made sense to me. I kept going from there."

"That's really interesting. Do you have examples of your work?"

Peregrine blinked in surprise. "You want to see my artwork?"

"Definitely."

"Okay, I guess." She went to the voicecom, input some commands, and pulled up a file. "Here, you can flip through."

The first image showed a Greek god. It was nice, but the hair didn't look right and the eyes were dead. As Emiko continued through the images, she saw a marked improvement in scope and realism.

The final image showed side-by-sides of a dark-skinned Rescan girl and a pale-skinned Sarkavian man. She leaned in closer. "Wait, are those—"

"The same person, in different makeup" Peregrine confirmed.

"Wow. That's amazing." Her eyes went from picture to picture, trying to pick out similarities, but it truly looked like two different people.

"Incredible. Next time I tail Hawk to the bar, I should have you transform me."

The hard cast of Peregrine's face softened. "You followed Hawk?"

"Yeah. Ended up drinking with him."

"How'd that go?"

Emiko smiled. "It didn't start out great, but I think it was a first step."

"Is that what this is?"

"I didn't consciously plan it that way, but maybe. I don't have many people I can talk to about these things. People like us are kind of isolated."

At that last word, Peregrine's eyes cut to her and they shared a long look. Emiko felt like what she said resonated strongly with Peregrine.

Was she from a place that had made her feel isolated?

"I guess we'll have to figure out how to talk to each other

about things that we can't talk to others about." Peregrine frowned, but it didn't seem like a displeased frown. More like a thoughtful one.

Emiko supposed she'd need to become versed in the frown stylings of her teammate. "I guess we will."

"Why not talk to your hot roomie?" Peregrine asked. "I would have expected you to go to him with your worries."

Emiko laughed, then quickly sobered when she remembered her dilemma of mixing her work and personal life.

"Uh oh. Did things go wrong? Maybe I have a shot with him now." Peregrine's face didn't convey humor, but Emiko was pretty sure that was a joke.

"Every couple has disagreements," Emiko said. "I got the feeling Hawk's single, though. Maybe you could try him."

Peregrine waved a hand. "Hairy man-beast is not my style. I like someone a little more polished."

Emiko laughed in surprise. Now she was certain Peregrine was joking. "Hairy man-beast! I like that one. Maybe that can be our code name for him."

"Works for me."

A comfortable silence settled over them, and Emiko decided it was a good time for her to go. Better to leave on a high note. "I should get to bed. My first class is early. Thanks for letting me in."

She said it so her words could be interpreted simply, as just meaning letting her into the room. Really, she meant it more meaningfully.

Peregrine merely nodded. "We'll see each other again soon, I'm sure."

"No doubt. I keep waiting for someone at command to decide they want us to go steal something just to prove we can."

"That would be cool. I hope they do."

Again, Emiko wasn't sure if that was a joke or not, so she just gave a proper bow and hurried out.

Back in her own dorm, Emiko wasn't sure how to feel about Raptor not being there. Relief and disappointment battled each other for supremacy, but neither won.

She sighed, grabbed her things, and took them down the hall to shower and brush her teeth.

Afterward, she double-checked the voicecom to make sure he hadn't left her a message. He hadn't.

Well, maybe it was best for them to take some time to think about their situation. They'd have to figure this out before going on serious missions.

Knowing that didn't make falling asleep alone feel any less lonely.

Raptor didn't return the next day, either. She sent him a message to make sure he was okay, and he briefly responded that he was.

She didn't like this feeling between them, or not speaking, but she needed time to think about things.

"Should we break up? End our romantic relationship?" she asked Whelkin after their training session.

"What do you think?" he asked.

"I don't know. That's why I'm asking you. Can it work for people to train and work together, and have a romantic relationship?"

"For some, it can. For others, it wouldn't. There's no rule on this, and your situation is hardly unique. Though most couples get together after being put on a team together, and having time to bond that way."

She pulled her ponytail loose, then regathered it and secured it again. "Does that make us less likely to work?"

He sighed. "Again, I don't know. My advice is to not make any decisions yet. See how things develop. Maybe the relationship between you two will help your team. Or maybe it will be a problem. All you can do is figure it out as you go."

"Yeah. I guess."

"You have to be careful, though. Your job is to look after the team. Right now, that means getting to know one another and earning each other's trust. Teammates have to have unfailing faith in one another. It requires a deeper trust than you can imagine. Don't let anything get in the way of that. *Anything.*"

"Right."

She walked slowly back to her dorm. It would be empty, and she wasn't eager to be there by herself.

Why did everything have to fall on her shoulders? Why didn't the others bear any responsibility in building their relationship?

Because she was the leader. It always came back to that.

Maybe she wasn't cut out to be the leader.

Emiko woke to the soft sound of her door closing. She bolted upright.

Whelkin stood there, dressed in black from neck to toe. He thrust something black at her. "Here. Get dressed. Hurry."

She waited a moment for him to leave, but he didn't.

"I said hurry."

She turned her back to him, shucked off her pajamas, and pulled on the snug, stretchy outfit. It was all one piece, so getting into it was a little tricky, but once she had it all tugged into place, it was surprisingly comfortable.

He handed her a comport, indicating that she should secure it in a small pocket designed for that very purpose at her waist. "Let's go."

She fought the urge to ask questions. He would tell her what she needed to know when he chose to.

She'd have to get used to that.

He hustled her across campus. She recognized Hawk's dorm as they approached it. Once inside, Whelkin reached into the bag on his shoulder, rummaged around, then pulled out another black outfit. This one much larger. He handed it to her, along with a comport.

"Go to Hawk's room and summon him exactly the way I summoned you. Override his door with zeta-three-three-alpha-nine. Go."

She spun toward Hawk's room, steeling herself to order him around the way Whelkin had done to her.

Blowing out a breath, she punched in the override code and the door opened. Hawk rolled off his bed and popped up, fists ready.

"Stand down," she ordered. She thrust the outfit at him. "Put this on. Hurry."

His lips pressed together and he stared her down. He wouldn't do it. What could she do?

But then he took the clothing from her hands, raised an eyebrow at her, then shrugged.

He apparently enjoyed sleeping in the nude, and she struggled to avoid showing any reaction. She imagined Peregrine and tried to emulate her.

After yanking on some underwear, Hawk wrestled himself into the garment. With his bulk, he had a harder time of it than she had. In another circumstance, she'd have found his contorting, wriggling, and pulling funny.

"What's the deal?" he asked as she led him back out to Whelkin.

Since Whelkin had said nothing to her, she remained silent as well. Besides, she didn't know what the deal was any more than Hawk did.

They repeated the process with Peregrine, and, finally, Raptor.

She felt strangest about entering his room and watching him change. With Hawk and Peregrine, it had been about doing her job. With Raptor, there was a lot of other stuff between them.

Then there they were. Four brand-new operatives and one experienced one. Whelkin remained silent as he led them through the night to a groundcar. They saw no one else along the way. Campus was deserted at that hour.

They rode in silence, not knowing where they were going. Whelkin drove, Emiko sat up front with him, and the other three sat in the back seat.

Emiko tried to keep her shoulders relaxed and maintain a calm, collected attitude, but tension seemed to twist the air around her. She wasn't sure how much of that was her, and how much of it she was picking up from her new teammates.

Two of whom were barely more than strangers to her. How were they supposed to work together?

Her tension lifted when they got to their destination. Or maybe it didn't lift so much as got crushed by excitement.

They'd arrived at an airfield.

Not a high-tech airfield, with towers and miles of concrete and a carefully choreographed ballet of arrivals and departures.

A squat little building sat alongside a single runway.

Oh, this looked like fun.

From her companions, she sensed increasing unease. A guilty feeling of glee glowed in her belly. She was going to enjoy this. Maybe that meant she was twisted, but she suddenly could not wait to get started.

Whelkin hadn't turned off the groundcar, but he turned to them. "This is where you four get out. Go to slip three. This has everything you need." He handed Fallon a tiny infoboard. She'd never seen one so small.

Cool. Was this spy gear?

Whoops. The device was not the important part. "Yes, sir," she snapped. "Roll out, team!"

That was awesome. She hoped she'd get the chance to say that again.

She had that exhilarated feeling again. That sensation, bubbling up from her toes to her knees, then electrifying her guts all the way up through her chest. The adrenaline. A sense of being alive that everyday life just did not bring.

She led them to slip three. As soon as she saw the aircraft, she had to contain her glee.

"Prelin's ass," Hawk said with a mix of wonder and horror. "What's that?"

"Single engine fixed-wing prop plane. Four-seater. Model number X5620. Maximum weight, one thousand and ten kilograms. Maximum speed, one hundred and seventy knots."

He looked mildly consoled. "So, you've flown one before, then?"

"Nope. But I know all the specs." She ran her hand down the plane's sleek exterior, then reached for the door.

"I feel like that's unlikely." He moved no closer to the craft. "Why would you have this particular model memorized when you've never flown one? This thing doesn't look special, except for being ancient."

"It isn't. I've memorized all models of airworthy craft currently in service with the PAC. Also, many historical craft no longer in use."

He stared at her. "Why?"

"Personal interest." She tapped her temple. "Also, an eidetic memory, more or less. I don't tend to forget things I've studied."

"Well, that must be pretty damned convenient come test time."

She grinned at him. "It doesn't hurt." She opened the single door to the craft. This was its one real design flaw, in her opinion. The other side had an emergency exit door that could be kicked out, but for normal loading and unloading, it all had to happen via the one door. "Hop in. Hawk and Raptor in the back. Peregrine, you're up front with me."

Hawk looked at the plane, then back at her. He heaved a sigh. "Fine, Fallon. But if you crash, I'm going to be super pissed."

He climbed in after Raptor, settling into the seat with all the calm of a rabid bear.

Fallon settled herself into the pilot's seat, then looked at the infoboard. It had been simplified, and it was a no-brainer to activate the recorded message.

She held it to the side to allow her teammates to see the screen, and turned up the volume.

"Greetings, Avian unit. Congratulations on your first team mission. It won't be easy. You're to proceed to the following coordinates. There's a meeting set up for you with a local crime boss by the name of Lowell. Act like you know what it's about. Your task is to find out what his most illegal product is, and purchase it. You'll find an account number on this infoboard with fifty thousand cubics in it. Once the transaction is complete, we'll have what we need to get him off the streets. This is the culmination of months' worth of investigation and undercover work, so don't screw it up. Good luck. Krazinski out."

Fallon glanced around at her team. Peregrine looked as inscrutable as always. Raptor looked thoughtful. Hawk looked pleased.

"All right," Hawk said. "Criminal activity. You all can just stand back and let me take care of this one."

"Pretty sure we're all supposed to participate," Peregrine answered drily.

"Whatever." Hawk shrugged. "How about you get this bucket in the air, Fallon? I'd like to get back to bed for a couple of hours, so let's get this done."

She didn't respond to him. Instead, she got out, checked the plane over physically, then requested permission from the port authority to begin her taxi down the runway.

All things considered, she shouldn't have been surprised that the response was to give her immediate clearance to taxi. She was just used to going into the queue and waiting her turn.

Everything was changing for her.

"This is where we put our headsets on," she informed her passengers. She demonstrated putting the mic right above her lips.

"Everyone functional? Things are about to get loud."

"Check," Peregrine said.

"Check," Raptor echoed.

"Check," Hawk added. "But I really hope you know what you're doing."

She opened the craft's door, shouted, "Clear!" and, after waiting a moment, activated the propeller.

The explosive sputter of the propeller beginning then settling into rhythm felt so right to her, it was like a homecoming.

She guided the tiny plane to the runway, then began the taxi. She gradually picked up speed, got into the optimal range, then left the Earth.

No matter how many times she did this, or in what vessel, she felt the heady sensation of buoyancy. Using camber and propulsion to slip the bonds of gravity felt like magic, no matter how many times she did it.

Doing it in such a small craft, where the sensations were stronger and empty air was just beyond her in any direction, only intensified the thrill.

Not so for her teammates. Once she got to a cruising altitude, she assessed her crew. Though Peregrine seemed to take it in okay, when she glanced behind, Raptor looked tense and Hawk looked downright pale.

"We're good," she assured him. "I've got this."

"I hope so," Hawk answered as she turned back to keep watch over her instruments.

She had actual instruments, not just digital readouts. She felt like she was back at the origin of Earth flight, with the Wright brothers.

Fine, so the technology at her fingertips was centuries beyond those guys, but it felt thrillingly primitive to her. Back to the basics.

Sadly, the designated coordinates were only an hour away. She contacted flight control of the small commuter airport and circled until she received clearance to land on the first of the two runways.

The ground rushed up at them, since the angle of the runway required a steep descent. She adjusted for the wind and, having gotten a good feel for the craft, nailed the landing, putting it right down on the number *one*.

The feeling of jubilance and satisfaction was like no other.

She taxied to the slip assigned to her by the authority, cut the engine, and watched the propeller come to an abrupt halt.

"Welcome to our destination," she said as she pulled her headset off. "Wherever we are."

She opened the door and got out, which allowed Peregrine to slide out, then Hawk and Raptor.

Raptor gave Fallon a grin as he got out. She smiled back, grateful. Whatever else was going on between them, she knew he'd be supportive.

Maybe that was all she really needed to know.

She consulted the infoboard. "We're going to need a taxi. Our meet point is two miles away. Hawk, you're going to be on point for this. Are you familiar with this Lowell guy?"

Hawk crossed his arms. "Heard of him. Never met him."

"How do you suggest we make the approach?"

"First off, you and this guy," he pointed at Raptor, "will need a place to hang out. Not only is it weird for four people to go to something like this, but he looks like he's headed to a preppy frat boy dress-up party."

Raptor's eyebrows shot up and he opened his mouth to say something.

Fallon put her hand on his arm. "You're right, four would be suspicious. We'll stake out a place to wait." She looked to Raptor. "Think you could find a system to hack into so we could keep track of them?"

Raptor frowned in thought. "Probably, so long as they carry something that will ping me with their location."

"Like a comport?" Peregrine asked. "The ones we have should be clean and untraceable."

"Yeah, but if they take it from you, I'll be out of luck. Too bad we don't have something they wouldn't know to take."

"I'll work on that for future missions," Peregrine said. "For now, we'll have to hope the comport works."

Hawk nodded. "We can handle whatever happens in there."

"Hang on," Raptor said. "How do you know you two can handle it, but we couldn't?"

Hawk met Raptor's gaze. "I didn't say you couldn't. Thing is, I don't know what you can do. I know this one can handle herself." He jerked a thumb at Peregrine. "I've seen her fight, and she grew up fighting for what she got, just like I did."

They all looked to Peregrine, whose eyes had widened slightly. "What makes you think that? I never told you anything about how I grew up."

"One survivor knows another. We're not like them."

"Maybe I didn't start out that way," Peregrine answered, her voice soft but with a hard edge. "But who are you to tell me who I am now?"

She stepped toward him, looking ready for a fight.

Fallon stepped between them. "Now's not the time for this. You want to debate our toughness or see who's left standing after a fight, fine. We'll do that later. But right now, we have a job to do. Got it?"

She stared each of them down, including Raptor.

They all gave her grudging nods.

"Good. Let's get ourselves into the right neighborhood and have a good look around. We'll figure out where Raptor and I will monitor you from. No talking about all this on the ride there, though. There's no telling who the driver knows around here."

Hawk gave her a nod, and she noted his look of satisfaction. He liked that she'd thought of that.

Good. She needed him to trust her judgment. She'd just have to impress him again, maybe a couple thousand times, until she had his confidence.

The ride over was nearly silent. The driver was a surly looking man who thankfully didn't engage in small talk. They asked to circle the downtown area a couple times, then had him pull over at the curb in an entirely nondescript spot. He didn't ask any questions.

As discussed, Hawk and Peregrine got out first, walking to the left. After waiting three minutes, Fallon paid the driver, then she and Raptor walked to the right.

She put her arm around his and leaned in, pretending to be just a couple out for the evening. She wished they weren't wearing the similar all-black outfit. It felt conspicuous. Why had Whelkin chosen it?

They went into a late-night café, ordered fancy coffee drinks, then sat down at a table with a voicecom display.

"This isn't my favorite way to work," he muttered, quietly enough to avoid being overheard by the couple on the other side of the café.

"It's all we've got. We have to work with it."

After two long minutes, he said, "I've got them. Cross-referencing their location with the city blueprints." After a pause, he said, "It's a big building. They're along an exterior wall. I wish I could tell how many people were in there."

"Can you patch into some system in that building?" she asked.

"Trying. I don't have any of my usual short codes or codebreaking programs." He made a sound of annoyance. "Their security system is locked down decently well."

"Can you break through it?"

"Of course. It's just a matter of how long it will take."

Minutes ticked by, and she worried that they would be no help to Hawk and Peregrine. She didn't like the idea of them being in there with some bad dude without having eyes on them. They didn't even have an escape plan.

She grew increasingly doubtful of their decisions up to that point when Raptor finally hissed, "Yes!" under his breath. "Here. Look."

The image was distant, but she could clearly make out Peregrine and Hawk sitting at a table with a bald guy.

She wished she could hear an audio feed, or at least read the body language, but neither was possible. "What about the other rooms? Are there a lot of people there? Anything weird going on?"

Raptor switched from camera to camera, showing a smattering of people, most of which seemed to be doing warehouse work. Moving inventory around, packing crates, and so forth. Nothing that looked nefarious.

Unless, of course, their inventory was something illegal.

She guessed it was.

When they switched back to the feed showing Hawk and Peregrine, he had stood from the table and was making large gestures with his arms.

Uh oh. That didn't look good.

She and Raptor exchanged a glance.

At what point should she go in after them? She couldn't do it too soon or she'd risk making a dicey situation into a horrible one. She'd have to wait until she knew for sure things had gone wrong.

She needed to trust that Hawk was the best person equipped to handle the situation right in front of him. This was why he'd been recruited.

The bald guy stood up. Emiko bit her lip.

The guy slapped Hawk on the back. Hawk slapped him back. Then he slid his arm around Peregrine and the pair casually walked to the exit.

"Did they do it?" She didn't mean to say it out loud, but she had.

The guy didn't follow them. Raptor switched to an exterior camera and they saw their teammates strolling down the street, back toward the spot they'd left the first taxi.

"Signal the comport, tell them to walk to the end of the lane. We'll pick them up there," she told him.

After a moment, he said, "Done."

"Good. Let's go."

"I DON'T like this guy's style," Hawk scowled as soon as he got in the taxi.

"Sorry, sir?" The driver peeked at him over his shoulder, looking nervous.

"Not you," Hawk qualified.

"Ah. I see. Destination?"

Emiko raised her eyebrows at Hawk in question. "Blue Nine."

She tried to figure out if that was a street name, a section of town, or a business name. If only she'd had a chance to study up on the city beforehand.

They pulled up in front of a bar, which made sense. After Emiko paid the driver and the groundcar drove off, Hawk filled them in.

"We're to sit at the bar and wait for someone to approach. We'll make half payment, get the location for the pickup, and pay the rest on delivery."

"Seems sketchy," Raptor said.

Emiko nodded. She was thinking the same thing.

"It's sketchy as hell," Peregrine muttered.

"Sure, but it's not that unusual," Hawk said. "Right now, they're trying to dig up info on us. No doubt they're running our images across all their facial recognition databases to see if they can trace us to rivals or authorities. A meet like this is a common stall tactic to give them some time to decide if they really want to deal with us."

"Or they could be planning an ambush," Peregrine added.

"Sure," Hawk agreed with a shrug. "But it's not really an either-or situation. Even if they decide we're okay to deal with, that doesn't mean they won't try to kill us once they have the money. That's business."

"Great," Emiko said sourly. Not that she'd expected any better.

Hawk gave her a hard pat on the shoulder. "Buck up, Fallon. This is what you signed up for."

She nodded. "You two hang out just outside the door for five minutes. Then take your places at the bar. We can't exactly be subtle about being your backup in here while dressed like you, so we'll follow you shortly after."

"Got it." Hawk put his arm casually around Peregrine and they leaned against the wall of the bar, looking like a couple enjoying their time together.

"He's good at that," Emiko noted.

"I'm sure he's had practice," Raptor noted. "Where are we headed?"

"Two blocks back, I saw a secondhand store. We should be able to get what we need there."

Inside the shop, she looked past the luggage, musical instruments, decorative items, and small furniture. She went straight for the four racks of clothing.

Since he'd be the tougher one to fit, she looked at the men's rack first. All she could find that would accommodate his wide shoulders was a light-blue button-up shirt with long sleeves. It would have to do. She removed it from the rack and shoved it at him, then moved to the smaller-sized women's clothing.

She ignored the skirts and dresses, since she didn't want to take off her jumpsuit. Whatever she wore would go over it.

She found a pair of wide-legged beige pants, and guessed they would work. To go with them, she selected a tailored white blouse with black details along the collar and cuffs.

"I'll be back." The dressing room was along the interior wall. Trying on the pants, she found that the length was okay, but the waist was a little loose. She pulled the blouse over her head and frowned at herself in the mirror. It was obvious she was wearing black underneath, but it would pass as an undershirt.

Good enough.

On the way to the cashier, she grabbed a belt. "We'll take these."

She snapped the tags off the pants and shirt she wore, and set the belt and man's shirt on the counter.

On the way out, she threaded the belt through the loops of the pants, and Raptor buttoned up his shirt.

He looked nice in light-blue.

They sidled into the bar and sat at a table that provided a view of Hawk and Peregrine as they sat at the bar.

Emiko studied the menuboard on their table. "I'm getting sake. Do you want to share?"

Raptor grimaced. "I've never had a taste for it, but I can pretend."

She smiled. "That's the job, right?"

She punched in the order, then felt like it wasn't enough.

Some food seemed like a good idea. She added two steamed pork buns to the order.

The buns seemed like a safe bet. A place like this wouldn't make them fresh, so they'd come straight from the package and go into the heat-ex.

They probably wouldn't get food poisoning.

In surprisingly short order, a server appeared, delivered the serving flask of sake with two small cups, and a plate that held both steamed buns.

Raptor reached for the flask, and moved it toward his cup.

"You should fill my cup. Then I fill yours."

He froze. "Oh. Sorry. Why?" He did as instructed, filling her cup, then returning the flask to the table.

"Tradition. Manners. It's a social bonding thing, showing goodwill toward each other." She poured the slightly chilled sake into his cup.

"I see. I guess you can tell I'm not from around here."

"No." She smiled to soften her sarcastic tone.

She was curious about his past, and where he came from, but she wouldn't ask. Their first lives were off limits.

Likewise, he didn't ask her about her background. She could tell he wanted to. It made the moment awkward. Their first lives contained too much information that could hurt one another, along with whoever was part of those first lives.

Some things were too dangerous to know.

She sipped from her sake cup, then bit into her steamed bun. It was hot, sweet, and spicy simultaneously. Darn good for food from a packet.

"Is it safe?" Raptor asked, looking skeptical.

"Not bad at all."

He took a cautious bite, shrugged, and took a bigger one.

They ate the food, then sat chatting and sipping their sake. Whoever was meant to meet up with Hawk and Peregrine, they were being slow about it.

Did that mean trouble was headed their way? If they didn't perform well on this first team mission, it wouldn't reflect well on them.

A full half hour after Emiko arrived, a burly guy with a round belly approached Hawk. He sat on the stool next to him. After a brief discussion, he presented an infoboard, which Hawk took. Transferring half the funds, presumably. They talked for a couple minutes longer, then the man departed.

Five minutes later, Hawk and Peregrine slipped out of the bar.

"Should we?" Raptor asked.

"We'll wait for his signal," she said, taking another sip of sake. She'd actually swallowed very little of the alcohol. She didn't want any of her reflexes dulled. Mostly, she just pretended.

The signal came a few minutes later. Her comport vibrated against her hip.

Meet us at the airport. So far, so good.

"Roll out," she said, standing and smoothing her secondhand blouse.

Raptor waited until they'd exited before nudging her and saying, "You're enjoying those power phrases, aren't you, Fallon?"

She smirked. "Yeah, I kind of am."

He summoned a taxi and then off they went, back to the airfield.

When their car had driven away, they looked for the other half of their team. They found them on the other side, past the buildings and approaching the aircraft slips.

"Nice outfits," Hawk said, looking them over.

"Just wait," Emiko retorted. "Next time, I'll put you in the costume."

He grinned at her. "You can try."

She wouldn't tell him so, but she liked his smile. It was one half genuine amusement, one quarter ego, and the last quarter was pure hedonism.

Despite herself and their situation, she started to like him a little.

"What's our status?" she asked.

"Waiting. I suggest you two go get the plane ready, and keep eyes on us. There's no telling what will happen at this point. Could be fine. Could be anything but fine. This is the fun part." Hawk's eyes glowed with a maniacal light she instantly recognized.

The way she felt about flying and fighting was how he felt about dealing with criminals.

Interesting.

Although they were different, it seemed they had at least a couple things in common.

"Agreed. We'll be watching. If you need help, signal us by lifting your right hand above your head."

Hawk nodded.

Raptor added, "Just be careful not to give any super high fives or anything by accident."

Hawk grinned at him.

Even Peregrine smirked.

They all shared a look. This grouping might just work as a team, after all.

She saw the realization in all of their eyes, too.

They walked through relative gloom until they got to the aircraft, which had better lighting. She had enough illumination to check the exterior of the plane over, ensuring all of its structures were intact.

Such a small, basic craft had none of the fail-safes of more modern designs. A small defect could be the difference between a successful trip and a fiery death.

She wouldn't tell the others about that.

Once inside the craft, she got in touch with the authority, and informed them of their impending departure, though they weren't ready as of yet.

She received clearance to depart at her leisure.

At her expression, Raptor asked, "What?"

"That's not normal. Even at night, even at a little field like this, you're always told to wait for specific clearance."

"Someone's cleared the way for us," he surmised.

"Yeah."

"I guess we should get used to living a different way. Being connected to people who can arrange things."

"Being expected to wander out into the night and deal with criminals," she added.

"We could always quit," he said.

They looked at each other and laughed.

"Wait, look," she said.

Two men were approaching Peregrine and Hawk, carrying a large metal container. Each held a handle on either side.

"What do you think is in there?" he whispered.

"Don't know. Drugs? Illegal medical supplies? Stolen art?"

"I hope it's art," he said as they watched Hawk and Peregrine talk with the men. "It would be more interesting, don't you think?"

She didn't answer. She was waiting, watching to see if Hawk raised his hand above his head. He talked with his hands, making expansive gestures, and each time his hands rose, she felt her adrenaline spike.

But no signal of trouble.

The guys set down the container and stepped away. After Hawk looked inside, reaching in and apparently rummaging about, he nodded, and an infoboard was presented to him.

He touched it, and it seemed like the deal was done.

Emiko stayed on alert, waiting for more people to come out of the shadows. She had her hand on the door, ready to burst out at any second. She'd already chosen the path she'd run.

But nothing. The men disappeared, and no others arrived.

Disappointment pooled in her stomach, but she denied its

existence. It would be stupid to hope for trouble. Better that things went down easy. She shouldn't be looking to try out her skills in a real-life situation. That was foolish.

Hawk moved to pick up the crate, but Peregrine made a sharp gesture and picked it up herself. He followed her, his eyes roving, watching for trouble.

But no trouble came.

Emiko got out and had Hawk keep watch while she and Peregrine loaded the container into the exterior cargo compartment. It was tight, just barely fitting. At least that meant she wouldn't have to strap it in to prevent it from shifting.

"How heavy is it?" she asked. She doubted it would affect the handling of the plane much, but it was a good idea to know.

Instead of answering, Peregrine stepped close, put her arms around Emiko's waist, and lifted her several centimeters above the ground. She gave a test bounce, then put her down again.

"A little more than you."

Emiko stared at Peregrine in surprise.

"What?" Peregrine asked. "I wanted an accurate basis of comparison."

Hawk barked out a laugh, and while Peregrine's face remained solemn, Emiko was pretty certain she was amused.

At least she had some sense of humor, even if it was an odd one.

"Fine. Let's go." She did an exterior inspection of the plane while the others got in. Once she was confident the ship was flightworthy, she climbed into the craft.

As she closed the door, bright light nearly blinded her.

"What's that?" Raptor tried to peek through his fingers to see.

"Stop there! You're under arrest for smuggling illegal items. Come out of the aircraft with your hands up."

"Prelin's ass, it's the local authorities," Hawk groaned.

"I can't see," Peregrine complained.

Emiko had about five seconds to decide. Surrender or make a run for it?

Of course they'd run for it. She didn't need to see to find the runway. She turned on audio readout of her position, and the plane roared to life.

In her mind, she pictured the schematic of the airfield, with its latitude and longitude markers. She goosed the throttle, throwing them forward much faster than she normally would ever go on the tarmac, and made it to the runway in short order.

Now turned away from the lights, she could open her eyes.

"Stop!" The loudspeaker ordered. "If you do not, we will be forced to open fire."

They'd shoot them down?

"Keep going," Hawk advised. "They're not going to shoot."

"How do you know?" Even as she asked, she increased the speed, nudging them toward the minimum for takeoff.

"You've got a tail full of orellium. They're not going to set off a fireball like that."

Finally. Takeoff speed. She pulled up and the wheels left the ground, giving her that feeling of leaving her stomach below on the ground.

She loved that feeling.

She ascended hard, banked, and set off for their destination. As Hawk had promised, they did not get shot out of the sky.

"You sure that was a good move?" Raptor asked.

"Better than getting caught," Hawk answered. "Relax, preppy guy. Your girl did good."

Raptor sighed into his mic, which was an obnoxiously grating sound. "I'm not preppy. That has never been my life."

"Whatever." Hawk sounded unperturbed. "You look like it."

"Yeah, well you look like a bear that's escaped from a nature preserve," Raptor shot back.

Emiko recognized this kind of exchange. She'd seen guys do

the same sort of insulting one another when what they really meant was approval.

Hawk laughed. "Thanks. I try."

After the initial thrill of escape faded, Emiko spent the rest of the flight wondering what awaited them upon landing. Would they just be taken into custody then?

After executing another textbook landing, she eased the plane into the slip she'd been assigned by the airport authority.

She let out a deep breath as she removed her headset. "Okay. Let's go see what's next."

Whelkin appeared out of the darkness, momentarily alarming her before she tamped down the urge to throw a punch.

She'd have to work on that.

A man and a woman, dressed in black like the rest of them, appeared behind Whelkin. He directed them toward the cargo.

"You four are with me. Inside for debriefing."

Emiko hadn't expected a warm greeting or even a, "Good job!" but the matter-of-factness of his demeanor felt a little underwhelming after their success.

He led them into a small room, similar to the one she'd sat in with Raptor and Captain Martinez before their test mission.

The similarity was so strong, she suspected PAC intelligence, or some division of it, operated this place. That would explain why there had been no local authorities when they arrived. Somehow, that had been handled.

Whelkin gestured at the chairs, and after they'd seated themselves, he sat. "Describe your mission, including why you made the choices you did."

An hour later, after relaying every excruciating detail and choice they'd made, Emiko felt worn out.

"Why did you leave two able-bodied members behind, rather than take them in with you, as a show of force?" Whelkin asked Hawk.

"For one thing, dirty dealings are not a group activity," Hawk answered. "One or two people, tops. Four would be strange. Also, it's better to have people they don't know about keeping tabs on you."

Whelkin nodded, then looked to Peregrine. "Why didn't you take a more active role? You didn't contribute a lot to this endeavor."

Peregrine didn't flinch. "Because others had more experience in the particular situations we encountered. I'd rather follow the lead of people who understand the situation."

Now he looked to Emiko. "And why did you order pork buns?"

She'd been expecting a question about her piloting choices, or splitting up the team. "Because no one sitting at a table in that bar was just drinking, and I didn't want to stand out."

Finally, Whelkin smiled. "Excellent, all four of you. You didn't do it exactly as I would have, but you used the right logic for all your decisions. You did well together. Any questions?"

Emiko had lots of questions. She just didn't think she'd get answers to them. Most likely, all she could do was wait until command was ready to reveal things.

"All right then. I do have this little bit of news." He handed an infoboard to her. "Your name has been corrected. You're officially Falcon now."

"Nah, that just sounds wrong," Hawk said. "You should change it back to Fallon. We've gotten used to it."

Raptor smiled. "I have to agree."

Even Peregrine nodded.

"It doesn't match. You're Avian unit." Whelkin looked mildly exasperated.

"Don't care." Hawk shrugged. "She's Fallon.

Whelkin shook his head and looked at her. "What do you say?"

She looked at Raptor, Hawk, and Peregrine, and felt a thread of a bond beginning to form. After seeing Hawk and Peregrine in action, she believed they could work together.

Letting them name her would help form that bond. "Yep. From here on out, I'm Fallon."

She handed the infoboard back to Whelkin.

He shook his head again, but smiled. "I'll see what I can do. It's an unusual request to change the name of a Blackout member."

Her breath froze in her chest.

He'd said it out loud. Until that moment, she hadn't been sure Blackout existed. It was a whisper. A rumor. A conspiracy theory, even, depending on one's politics.

She'd known she'd be a spec op or a black op. It had always been her plan. But being a member of Blackout took even that to a new level.

Whelkin broke the silence. "Yes, it's real. And now you're part of it. I hope you're prepared for that, since there's no going back now."

She exchanged looks with the others. They didn't want to go back. They were all in this, one hundred percent.

"All right," Whelkin said. "Let's get back to campus. You four need to get to your classes in the morning and carry on as usual. Remember, you're just college kids, dealing with the end of third year."

"Like we can forget," Hawk said. "Math is kicking my ass."

Fallon and Raptor laughed. Hawk was just so rough around the edges and tough. He was nothing like an officer should be.

And maybe that was a good thing.

Whelkin didn't look offended, though he could have taken exception to such a breach in protocol. He didn't insist on all the typical bows in informal situations, but talking back like Hawk had done just wasn't done.

"It kicked mine, too," he admitted. "Keep at it."

Two weeks later, Fallon had completed her classes. All that remained was to prepare for finals and the end-of-year championships that would determine the class rankings for skills like archery, hand-to-combat, and knife throwing.

She was no archer, but she intended to win the second two.

She and Raptor had settled into a somewhat different pattern. He stayed at his dorm some nights, and at hers some nights. Every now and then, she went to stay with him.

They got along as well as ever, and their chemistry remained strong. They'd fallen into a weird valley, though, of not knowing what to do about their relationship. Whether to forge ahead with it or just be teammates. Somehow.

She kept waiting for the answer to come to her, but it didn't.

Each night when she went to bed, she wondered if she'd be yanked awake and sent on another mission. So far it hadn't happened.

She had started joining Hawk at his favorite bar for drinks every two or three nights. She had a better handle on his personality now and his sense of humor was growing on her. She'd have to get used to some of his other habits, like profuse swearing and a habit of giving people a lecherous head-to-toe stare down.

"Tell you what," she said as she finished her flask of sake. The night of their first mission had given her a taste for it. "After the championships, when the year is completely over, I say we invite Peregrine and Raptor here and see who falls off their stool first."

He pursed his lips and nodded. "I like it. Let's do that. I hope you're not competing in any events I'm in, though, because you'll lose, and I don't want to hear you whining about it."

She laughed. "Lose? You have no idea."

He scoffed at her. "Little thing like you? You look like an origami championship would be too rough on you."

Now he was just screwing with her. He dwarfed her in size,

and she didn't have Peregrine's strong physique, but there was no mistaking that she was fit.

She rolled her eyes. "We can't all be built like an ox. Some of us have to do more with less."

He laughed. "Well, you give it your best."

She snorted.

It was fun, joking around with him.

"You and Raptor fighting?" he asked.

"No. Why?"

"He asked me out for pizza."

When she looked at him, he said, "Not like *that*. I mean, he's cute and all, but he's entirely hung up on you. But he asked if I was hungry, and I said yes, and he said he'd pay. So I made him regret that decision, because I can eat more than you can imagine."

"Believe me, I can entirely imagine it."

This time, he snorted at her.

"So, what did you talk about?" she asked.

"Eh. Nothing particular. He seems like a good guy. I won't hate knowing him."

"What about Peregrine?"

"I knew her a little before, and we grab some food now and then. We understand each other."

Hm. It seemed they were all hanging out together on different schedules. She supposed that was good, all of them forming their own relationships. They should all probably spend more time together. Maybe there was a sport they all liked or something.

"Now you've gone all thoughtful," he scowled at her. "What's with that?"

"I'm not," she denied. "Maybe I'm drunk."

"Hardly. I've seen you drink way more than that. For a little thing, you can pack it away okay."

She took that as a compliment. Hawk put great store by eating and drinking.

"What about me?" she asked.

"What about you?"

"Think you'll hate knowing me?"

He studied her over the rim of his glass. "Guess we'll see. I don't hate you yet, so that's promising."

"Still think I'm a spoiled rich girl?"

"Yes. But that doesn't mean you aren't other things, too. Just like I'm street trash and more things, too."

"Huh." She found that surprisingly pragmatic of him.

"What?" He frowned at her.

"When you put it that way, it sounds okay. Street trash or spoiled rich girl. Those things are relative." To him, she imagined she was a rich girl. "It's the other things we are that matter, right?"

"Yeah. So long as they overshadow the rest. That's what I think, anyway. But maybe I'm just making excuses for myself. Trying to sound better than I am."

It was her first glimpse into his true thoughts. The thoughts they all had, that they hid from others. Doubt, worry, fear.

"You're not." She pushed the pretzel knots at him. "I wouldn't share my pretzel knots with someone like that."

"They're my pretzel knots," he grumbled. But he grabbed one and stuffed it into his mouth, whole.

"I wouldn't share your pretzel knots with someone like that, either."

He grinned at her.

"Make me someone else."

Peregrine stared at Emiko. "What?"

"Do your makeup thing and make me look like someone else. I want to see how it works." She'd met Peregrine in her room, where her disguising tools were.

"Why?"

"First, because I need to have a sense of your abilities. Our job before didn't give you a chance to show what you can do. Second, because I should learn what it's like to be in costume. Surely it takes practice to be able to embody someone else."

Peregrine slightly pursed her lips. For her, it was a look of deep thoughtfulness. "Reasonable. I don't have a lot of time today, so I'll work with your existing facial structure, but I can do something more elaborate tomorrow."

"Okay. What should we do?"

Peregrine gave a sharp nod of decision, and Fallon felt a sudden sense of nervousness. What would Peregrine make her into?

"A glamourous holo-vid type," Peregrine decided.

"Me?" Fallon laughed. "I'm as girl next door as it gets. I'm not even the especially cute girl next door."

"I can make it happen, with your face and hair. You've got the body for it, though you're a little short. A shame I don't have a dress and high platform shoes for you to wear, to really get the feel of it. We'll have to improvise. That's the thing you need to learn—how to embody your character and move like they would."

"I can move like a holo-vid star," Fallon argued. "It's just walking and posing, acting like you're amazing."

"No. It isn't. Sit." Peregrine indicated the chair.

She sat.

Peregrine reached into her closet and pulled out a huge case. She set it on the desk, opened the lid, and it expanded to what seemed like three times its original size, with tons of little drawers and cubbies.

"Wow."

"Be still," Peregrine ordered, rubbing something on her face.

Other stuff followed that. Then more stuff of a different, yet also flesh-toned color. And then something berry-colored. Then powder. And then, somehow, more stuff.

It was exhausting. No wonder she didn't wear makeup.

"I'm going to use a wig, for the sake of time," Peregrine said. "Sit still and don't touch your face."

It wasn't easy. Her face felt weird. Her eyes felt kind of wet and gloopy around the edges. She wanted to find a mirror and sneak a peek, but didn't want to get in trouble.

So she obediently sat still and didn't touch her face.

Then Peregrine was pulling at her hair, pinning it up, and settling a big hairy blanket on her head.

It was itchy, and she immediately hated it. But she remained still.

Peregrine fussed with the thing, made adjustments and styled it, and finally stood back and stared at Fallon.

She nodded. "Okay. Have a look."

She handed Fallon a mirror.

"Wow." Fallon carefully touched her cheek, which somehow now had prominent cheekbones. Her eyes were huge, and round and *pretty*. Her lips were fuller, her mouth wider, and her nose looked narrower.

"How the hell did you do that? It's just makeup."

One edge of Peregrine's mouth raised slightly. Was that a smile? "It's bringing attention to the things you want to be seen, while camouflaging the things you want to keep hidden. That's all you. It's just highlighting the best parts."

She turned her head from side to side, pouted her lips, tilted her head and smiled. It was weird that the person in the mirror was her.

She smoothed her hands gently over the long, wavy locks around her face. It was a similar shade of black as her own hair, but this was fuller and silkier. Much longer and more luxurious.

"Now stand," Peregrine instructed. "Act like you're showing up at an important event."

Self-conscious, she put her shoulders back and took three steps across the space.

"Stop. You move like an anti-grav cart. You need to shift your weight with each step and put some swing in your hips."

"I can do that," Fallon said defensively. "You're just making me nervous."

"Show me."

She backed up to the door and let out a breath, remembering her hip-swinging stride from the tram station on Luna. She tried to replicate it.

"Better," Peregrine said. "But too young. Shorten your steps, take your time. You're there to be seen, so you're not in a hurry. Imagine yourself as molasses on a cold day. Sticky, slow, and heavy."

Fallon hated the analogy, but didn't say so. She focused on embodying molasses.

"Good. Almost passable. Work on it."

"How do you know this stuff?" Fallon asked.

"Study. A lot of it comes from just watching people. Seeing how subtle differences in how a person moves affects their appearance. I took some theater classes, too, both for emoting with the body and for costuming."

"Awesome. I'm impressed."

"Really? For a makeover?" Peregrine looked dubious.

"Well, that and how much you've put into studying it. It's great."

"Well, wait until tomorrow. I'll make you into something really amazing."

"I'm a little scared, when you say it like that," Fallon joked.

Again, that little quirk on one side of Peregrine's mouth.

"Anyway, I need to get going." Peregrine didn't reveal her plans, and Fallon didn't ask. Some things weren't her business.

"I'll see you tomorrow, then. I'm going to go try out this look." Fallon posed dramatically. At least, she hoped that was what she was doing.

FALLON SASHAYED across campus in the most in-character way possible. Her pants and shirt marked her as a student and were far from glamorous, but she still got plenty of attention.

She concentrated on her sticky molasses walk, elegant turns of the head, and a casual attitude that she hoped conveyed the impression she wasn't even trying to be this amazing.

Normally, people's eyes usually slid over her, probably not even registering her unless they had a reason to.

Today, people's eyes stuck to all her molasses, and they stared for the entire time they were in her view.

She didn't turn to see if they were still looking after she'd passed. She was far too fine for that.

She laughed, though, just thinking that. It wasn't the real her, but it was fun to pretend for just a little while.

At Raptor's door, she used the chime rather than the door code.

When he answered, he wore a polite smile. A confused look crept in, then realization hit. All this happened in two or three seconds, and she took great delight in it.

"Wow," he said, stepping aside so she could enter.

"That's what I said." She continued her molasses mosey up to his bed, where she sat primly and posed, looking up at him through her false eyelashes.

"That's amazing. It's like it's not even you. You look fantastic."

She affected an annoyed look and his eyes widened.

"Not that you don't always look fantastic. It's just a different... more understated kind of fantastic. More wholesome. Actually, I like that better." He nodded repetitively, as if that could convince her of his sincerity.

She laughed. "It's fine. I know I look great, and it's not my usual thing."

"You do look great usually. Strong and healthy and confident and cute. I like your usual look."

She smiled. "I said it's fine. I've never really been concerned with looks."

"And I've always liked that about you."

"Yeah?"

He sat down next to her and smiled. "Yeah."

"Have you eaten? Want to go get some dinner? Make everyone jealous you're with such a gorgeous woman?"

He laughed. "No way. People will think I'm cheating on you."

He ducked the pillow she swung at his head, and they both laughed.

"I like that we can laugh together and say how we really feel, even when it's not good," he said.

"Me too."

"Good." He leaned in like he would kiss her, so she leaned in, too. He whispered in her ear, "Let's order some food. I'm starving."

They laughed again.

8

"We're making progress," Fallon told Whelkin, sitting on the floor of the training room. "I wasn't sure at first, but we're going to make this work. I'm starting to like Hawk and Peregrine."

"Teams are put together very carefully," Whelkin said. "So I'm glad you're already finding common ground. What you need to focus on, though, is the championships. If you still want to win, that is. Whether you do or don't won't affect your career."

"When I got here, my goal was to be the best. To get the top marks in my classes, and to be first in my class. That goal has driven me the whole time I've been here. Not meeting it would be letting myself down."

He frowned at her. "You've never had to accept a loss?"

"Of course I have. But not often. And never on a specific goal."

"I see. You need to focus on training, then. Hawk and Peregrine won't be easy to beat. There are only a couple of others that might be able to challenge you three."

"I'm looking forward to seeing Hawk's and Peregrine's styles. I kind of wish we'd been able to train together."

"You'll do plenty of it in OTS. Don't worry about that. What you should consider is that Peregrine and Hawk didn't grow up fighting because they wanted to, like you. They started fighting early because they had to."

She'd suspected that they'd both come from rough backgrounds. "Why are you telling me that? We're not supposed to know about first lives."

"As their leader, I think it's something you need to understand about them. They will see things differently than you. They'll approach things differently. It will be up to you to recognize when to encourage them to follow their instincts and when to pull them back. It's your job to take care of them."

He leaped to his feet. "And that's your first class in becoming a commander. It's a short one, because all the most important ones are."

"Are you off to train one of them now?" she asked. "Maybe give them a pep talk, specific to them?"

He smiled. "Of course."

"Good. Teach them well." She stood and put her bag over her shoulder.

He nodded approvingly at her.

She slowly walked back to her dorm. Raptor was busy working on some major hacking something or other, so she had to decide what to do with the rest of her evening.

Earlier that day, Peregrine had transformed her into an old lady, complete with wrinkles and thin white hair with pink scalp peeking through. She'd given her lessons on moving slowly and carefully, too.

It had been fun, and Fallon had especially enjoyed scaring the crap out of Raptor by appearing at his door and pretending to be lost and confused.

He'd been endearingly sweet and kind, though. He was a good guy.

Though when she'd revealed herself to him, he'd bopped her

on the head pretty hard, before sitting on his bed and laughing his ass off.

He had a good sense of humor, too.

He was perfect, really. Perfect for her. And though they never said it out loud, she loved him.

But as Whelkin had said, she was responsible for him, too. As graduation loomed closer and closer, the deadline for their decision about their relationship also got closer.

She didn't see how she could love him the way she wanted to, and be able to command him and be responsible for him, too.

For that night, though, she just leaned into him, while she still could.

9

In the days leading up to the championships, the campus grew quieter. And more carefree. With finals over and rankings complete, many students not competing in the championships disappeared. Maybe they went home to enjoy a respite before whatever life handed them next. Or maybe they wanted to steal some time with a lover before they moved on to a job, a graduate program, or OTS.

It was a time of possibilities.

Fallon watched the change come across campus. She'd noticed it less in her previous years at the campus because she'd always been focused on what came next. Now she was able to see what was happening among the people she'd spent the last three years attending classes with, sitting on the quad with, and competing against.

Life on the quad bloomed. People played games, laughed freely, and lolled about on blankets.

Good for them. Fallon understood now the importance of relishing what you have, while you still have it. Of savoring the moment, because soon it would be gone.

Of living in the now.

She thought of herself entirely as Fallon now. It hadn't been too hard to make the shift. She hadn't been Emiko for that long. Names were like a hat you put on, depending on where you were going. Identities, she suspected, were the same.

At first, the name had been hollow for her, and she'd had to remind herself to use it. Now, she felt like she inhabited the name, like a new home she'd moved into and made herself comfortable within.

She spent time on the quad, too. Sometimes with Raptor, sometimes with Peregrine. Never with Hawk. She appreciated the vicarious happiness of her other fellow classmates, though she would never be like them.

They were the ones she would spend her life protecting. They, and others like them, were the PAC people who would do all the living and working and loving and dying while she was among the stars, doing who knew what kinds of terrible things.

Somebody had to. She was one of those somebodies. Raptor, Hawk, and Peregrine were those kinds of somebodies, too.

Achievers. Outliers. Heroes.

She laughed at the thought, even as Peregrine sat across from her, looking entirely unimpressed by the frolicking all around them.

Peregrine was hard, but not as hard as she appeared. Otherwise, she wouldn't appreciate all this as much as Fallon knew she did.

Fallon had all these tenuous connections to Peregrine and Hawk now, and it was up to her to keep building on that foundation. Making them stronger, as a team and as individuals, just as Whelkin had told her they'd need to be.

Better. Fallon refused to lose her teammates.

Peregrine sighed. "Look at all that perfectly good champagne they're spraying at one another. So stupid."

Fallon followed her gaze. "Wasteful, certainly. But what are they going to remember when they're fifty? The cost of the bottle or the joy of the moment?"

Peregrine lifted her hand to her mouth and chewed on the pad of her thumb. She did that during deep thought.

"Maybe," Peregrine admitted.

"Tell you what," Fallon said. "I'll buy you a bottle of whatever champagne you like after the championships. Come meet Hawk and me. We'll invite Raptor, too. It will be our own version of a last hurrah."

Peregrine's subtle half-smile appeared, and Fallon felt victorious.

Sometimes, the tiniest details mattered. Peregrine's micro expressions definitely counted among these. Every time Fallon earned one, she felt like she'd won a major award.

Peregrine didn't waste her expressions on just anyone.

"Are you ready?" Fallon asked. "For the championships, I mean."

Peregrine squinted up toward the fluffy clouds drifting lazily across the sky. "As ready as I'll get. Time's up."

"Yeah," Fallon echoed. "Time's up." With the weight of the future upon her, she understood what she had to do.

Raptor stayed in his quarters the night before the championships began. They both wanted space to focus.

Fallon respected him for valuing that above spending the night with her.

She'd limited her events to only hand-to-hand combat and knife throwing. They were what mattered most to her. Knife throwing was a small niche, but she was like the Robin Hood of knife throwing. She had no worries there.

Combat was another matter. Though she felt confident in her skills, she'd never had the opportunity to study her competition.

She didn't like being in the dark. She wanted all the information so she could assess it, weigh it, and decide on a strategy.

Instead, she had only her hard-earned skills and her wits.

She arrived in her loose-fitting black shirt and pants. She'd trained in such clothing since before she could remember, and it felt as comfortable as her own skin.

Many championships were open to the public. They were a social event, a coming-of-age ritual. Hand-to-hand combat was one of the few exceptions. The rationale was that judges had to be close and undistracted to render a decision. The reality was that the PAC had to hide their spoofing of identities.

Whoever won would be someone already chosen to move into hidden parts of the PAC. Therefore, the official winner would probably be someone no one knew.

Because it would be some actual first-life person. Or something. Who knew? It wasn't her place to ask. Someday, she was determined that it would be. For the moment, she wasn't even officially an OTS cadet.

Fallon didn't care how the PAC squared it all away. She only cared that she knew she'd won. She needed no public recognition. She just wanted to prove to herself that she was the best, and bring honor to her father.

He didn't even need to know about it. Honor was its own reward. She would know that his many years of training her and taking her to lessons and competitions had served its purpose.

Now, in the locker room outside the fight ring, she sat on the floor, her back against the lockers. She blew out a long breath, closed her eyes, and visualized success.

With each long inhale, she drew in positive energy. Every exhale expelled all negative thoughts, all doubts, all uncertainty. She had lived the best parts of her life after cleaning herself of negativity and bringing in only honesty, integrity, and life.

Her father had taught her this. She still pictured his smooth, long-fingered hands, as they gently held her tiny thumb and forefinger into the shape of infinity, of the universe, of everything and nothingness all at once.

Tears rolled out from behind her closed lids. He'd given her so much. Loved her so completely. It was because of him that she'd found it within herself to fight to where she was today.

She would bring him honor, no matter what it took.

"Emiko Arashi?" A soft voice intruded on her thoughts, and she opened her eyes.

The woman said, just as softly, "It's time."

THE FIRST ROUNDS WERE NOTHING. Laughable. Not worth a half-night's sleep, much less the deep focus she'd brought forth.

Her opponents were easy to knock down. Easy to pin. Easy to force into submission. They were only the poseurs. The ones whose egos made them think they had what it took.

She moved through three such rounds. Battles that didn't deserve the name. They didn't raise her pulse or make her think beyond a plus b equals c.

It was a farce.

Then came the ones who were more capable, with a few tricks but no dedication.

They were a farce, too.

And then came the real competition.

She only witnessed her own fights. After each, she returned to the same spot in the locker room to focus her energy.

Unknown face after vaguely recognized face appeared across from her. She kept expecting Raptor to show up on the other side of the ring, but he never did.

Someone else must have beaten him, because the quiet voice in the locker room told her she'd advanced into the finals.

Two fights, and she'd be the winner.

She'd fought thousands of times. Twice was nothing.

She focused only on that, and her confidence in her abilities. She expected these to be the most arduous fights of her life.

She was ready.

When she stepped out of the locker room, adrenaline seeped into her veins. She was ready for this challenge. Eager.

She stepped into the ring and there was Peregrine. Nearly twice her weight and with a blank stare.

Blank to other people. Fallon saw tiny flickers of pride, eagerness, and adrenaline.

No fear. No regret. Just like Fallon.

The bell rang.

Peregrine's reach was greater, and she was stronger. They circled around each other slowly, doing little test jabs and feints. They knew nothing about each other's fighting styles. Fallon didn't know whether to expect a boxer, a brawler, or a martial artist.

When Peregrine finally threw a real punch, with all of her weight behind it, she knew.

The woman was a boxer, or something like it. Her strikes had incredible power. If Fallon got on the wrong end of one of those hits, she'd be knocked out cold.

Fortunately, her style was like grease. She slipped aside. Sideways. Dodged. Used Peregrine's power to pull her off-balance. Waited for her moment.

It wasn't easy. Peregrine was explosive. Tough. And she could take a hit.

Finding that opening wouldn't be easy. How much stamina did Peregrine have? Such a big person expended a lot of energy. She could tire her out.

And she did. Fallon dodged, ducked, and slid aside, greasy as a bulkhead with a metric ton of solvent spread over it. She didn't risk taking any hits to gain an advantage because Peregrine's strikes were too forceful.

Finally, after a ridiculously long thirty-minute bout with no breaks, Peregrine slowed. She was tiring.

It was time.

Fallon watched for her opening. After another wicked strike that probably would have given her brain damage, Fallon ducked under it, leaped onto Peregrine, and forced her to the ground. She slipped sideways, her thighs around Peregrine's neck, and locked her ankles.

Either Peregrine tapped out or choked out. Once they were on the mat, those were the only two choices. As hard as Peregrine pulled at Fallon's knees, there was no getting loose.

She hit the mat three times, tapping out.

Fallon leapt to her feet, helped Peregrine up, and hugged her. Tears stung her eyes. She didn't know why. Peregrine gripped her right back in a huge bear hug.

"Break it up!" The referee shouted, pulling at them. He didn't know what he was seeing.

"It's okay," Fallon said, releasing her partner.

"We're good," Peregrine said, letting go.

They were both fighters, and partners, and from then on, they'd be fighting on the same side. Far more than the rush of winning, Fallon felt the satisfaction of belonging.

She returned to the locker room, sat again, and tried to return to her earlier state of zen. It didn't come as easily. She'd been seduced by the glow of belonging and acceptance. Peregrine had felt it, too.

Maybe it was better. Maybe she needed ego. In her mind's eye, she'd always seen the final fight going down a particular way. And when she was summoned for the final time to come to the ring, she knew she had been right.

The ant and the elephant. Fallon against Hawk. He gave her no hint of recognition of friendship. He glared at her, sweating, glistening, and bulging.

How the scrap was someone her age built like that? He was a

bloody tank.

No, a furious tank.

And he was here to win.

Fallon set her jaw. So was she.

She barely ducked out of the way of a punch. How was he so fast? He was too big to be that fast.

But he was. He was incredible.

As slick and evasive as she was, he grazed her with his strikes, over and over. Across the ribs. Across the cheekbone. She always turned aside, but just a millisecond too late.

She couldn't get her arms around his throat. Couldn't land that one, decisive strike to his temple. He was far too big to unbalance.

He had the upper hand. Still, she was quicker. She tried to tire him out like she had Peregrine, but the guy was a machine. His force never let up.

She had no choice but to look for a killing blow. The kind Whelkin had taught her to look for, to end a fight quickly when she was outmatched.

Except he'd taught Hawk the same techniques. She saw him guarding against her. Again and again, he made her fall back, ceding ground to him.

She was in trouble. This was no stalemate. This was him wearing her down.

She ducked, dodged, and wondered if this was what it felt like to lose something really important. She'd thought that if she worked hard enough, and never spared herself pain or doubt, she could always push through. It wasn't happening this time.

Then her shot appeared. Like the clouds of a storm suddenly parting and dark skies giving way to sudden, blinding sun, her opportunity appeared. He put every ounce of everything he had into a punch to her solar plexus, trying to take her down once and for all.

And he left his throat exposed. Just for an instant. Just long enough. She could launch a punch, straight up from her feet, through her toes, to uppercut right into his trachea.

He'd go down. Unable to breathe. She'd win. Emiko Arashi, or Fallon, or whatever the hell they wanted to name her, she'd be the champion.

Except.

Except she'd probably crush Hawk's trachea.

He'd probably be rendered unable to breathe.

Even though emergency support was on hand, they might not be able to help him.

She'd come to the academy to win. To be the best, no matter what. And here Hawk was, ready to punch her full force to take that from her.

A moment of clarity peeked through her singularity of purpose. Maybe it was zen, or maybe it was loyalty.

He was hers. Hers to protect. Her teammate, and someone who, undoubtedly, would be her protector in the future. Could she risk his life to win?

She took the shot, but slowly enough that she knew it wouldn't hit the target.

He blocked it with one arm and landed the blow to her chest with the other.

Time shattered around her. She didn't feel the impact of falling on her back. She felt only the inability to draw a breath. The inability to process anything around her. She rallied everything she had to gasp in a breath.

A horrible sound filled her ears, of her own breath. Big, gentle hands moved her onto her side. She coughed, gasped, and sputtered in the way a loser did.

Words were said, a champion declared, but Fallon heard none of it clearly. It was a vague impression she had on her periphery.

Strong arms lifted her, taking her away from the noise. She saw flashes of ceiling, floor, and lockers. And then faces. Hawk. Then Peregrine and Raptor approached, looking worried.

"I'm good," she rasped. Even to her own ears, she did not sound good.

A pouch of biogel was put to her lips. She wasn't dehydrated, but apparently that was all they could think of to do. She sipped at it, though she didn't want it. In the distance, she heard a disagreement, a growling threat, then ensuing silence.

Her chest eased up and she took her first, full, deep breath. Color rushed back into her world. After two more breaths, sound returned to normal.

"I'm good," she said again. She squinted at Hawk. "Did you just threaten the emergency medical team?"

He broke into a grin, relief lighting his eyes. "Yeah. I did. You just had the wind knocked out of you. You didn't need their bullshit."

She laughed, coughed, and laughed some more.

"Congratulations on winning," she said.

"No. You won. You just chose not to prove it to anyone else. But you and I know." His eyes were warm in a way she'd never seen before.

"You're mine to look out for," she said. "All of you. And I'm going to take care of you, no matter how much of my blood and bone it takes."

Tears came to her eyes again for no good reason, pissing her off. She wasn't someone who ever cried about anything. Ever.

"We'll take care of you, too." Hawk put his hand on hers. "Blood and bone."

Raptor added his hand. "Blood and bone."

Peregrine put hers on top. "Blood and bone."

Fallon put her other hand on Peregrine's.

They were a team. For the rest of their lives, however long that was, these were her three partners.

They were Avian unit. And they were going to kick so much ass.

Raptor, Hawk, and Peregrine attended the knife-throwing competition. Fallon easily won. She didn't even have to try hard, which was a bit of a disappointment.

But it made her heart swell to see her team cheering for her when she received her prize—a knife engraved with the name Emiko Arashi and the words *Grand Champion*.

"'*Arashi*' means 'storm', right?" Hawk asked after slamming down an entire glass of something vile at his favorite bar.

Oh, yes, she had held them to their promise of going out for drinks.

"Yes." She looked at him in surprise.

"Don't look so shocked," he groused. "I can look shit up."

She laughed and bought him another drink. It only seemed fair.

Then he bought a round for them all. "What are the odds that the top three fighters in our class are right here?" he asked.

Raptor shrugged, biting into a pretzel knot. "Probably not too terrible, all things considered."

Hawk frowned at him. "Shut up. I'm being poetic, here. Or metaphorical. Or...I dunno, some kind of fancy-pants thoughtful. Whatever."

Raptor grinned at him.

Hawk pointed at him. "And you keep that preppy-boy smile to yourself. I think you're just jealous that you're the only one here not among the top three."

Hawk looked at Peregrine and Fallon, then slanted a taunting look at Raptor, who laughed.

They laughed and ate and drank into the wee hours. Far later than Fallon's disciplined bedtime. But all rules needed to be bent sometimes, and she suspected that the further she went into the future, the more truth she'd find in that idea.

By the time she made it back to her dorm that night, with

Raptor in tow, she felt better than she wanted to. Not nearly as drunk as she'd hoped.

She had some unpleasant business to deal with still. With the championships over and graduation looming, she knew what she needed to do.

He knew it, too.

"I've been waiting for this," he said, sitting beside her on the bed without touching her.

"So, you know it's the right thing to do, right? I mean, we're on our way to becoming officers. Our time to be selfish is over. We have to think about the team now."

"Yeah," he said. His reply sounded more like a sigh than a proper word. "It's bigger than us now, isn't it?"

"Wasn't it always? You and I were never aiming for simple office jobs. Finding each other was a surprise along the way."

"A good surprise," he said.

"An incredible surprise," she admitted. "I never expected to have what we have. And when I found out we'd be on the same team, I was thrilled, thinking it didn't have to end. But…"

"But we have two other people to think about now. It's not just us."

"Yeah. How does that work? What if our relationship clouds our vision? Or unbalances our team?"

"I know. I've thought about it, too. Still."

"I know," she agreed. "It won't be easy for you and me to keep our distance. To just be partners. We have to try, though."

He rubbed a hand over his face, and she'd never felt worse in her life.

He put his arm around her and she realized that he would always be better than her. Not at fighting, but at being a good person. He would go along with this decision for the sake of the team, and her, and he'd still be kind to her.

She didn't deserve him.

He took a teasing tone she'd long since become accustomed

to. "We could always chuck it all. Go be freelancers. Me, a hacker, you, a high-profile bodyguard."

She made a sound, and even she didn't know if it was a laugh or a sob. "That's stupid. Why would we settle for less? I want to be the best."

"It wouldn't be less if we were *together*," he argued. "And we might even live to see old age. Does that not sound at all good to you?"

She pulled away, then sighed and leaned into him instead.

He wrapped his arm around her.

"I've aimed my whole life at being the best. Even though I know you're just joking, I can't help thinking about it. But as much as I care about you, I can't forget about how hard I've worked to get where I am. If I missed my opportunity, I might grow to resent you. Maybe even hate you. Besides, we have Hawk and Peregrine to think about. It's not just about us."

He rubbed her hand between both of his. "I guess that's it, then."

"I'm sorry. This is just the way I'm made."

"I know. I always knew that." He nudged her and smiled. "I just thought it was worth a try. To be sure. Now we know."

"Yeah. I guess." She didn't know if it was better to have considered chucking it all. It was too irresponsible, and yet, in a tiny way, tempting.

"After graduation, we'll have to find a way to be just partners."

"I know." Young Fallon raised her hands to cup his face. She leaned in and kissed him. "That's three weeks away, though. For now, we can just..." She trailed off, sliding into his lap and running her hands under his shirt. Raptor didn't argue with her plan.

GRADUATION DAY WAS GREAT, and exciting, and strange.

Her family couldn't come, given that she wasn't attending under a name they knew. If they looked that name up, they'd find her, along with all the regular statistics, and a dummy acceptance into OTS, but there was too much risk for exposure.

She didn't know how PAC command managed such things, but they must, somehow. Maybe someday she'd understand it.

Besides, her parents, thanks to their own backgrounds, probably knew how to read between the lines and hear the things that weren't said. They knew that she'd always had high aspirations. So instead of attending, they sent their congratulations and proud wishes via voicecom.

She could only wonder what Raptor, Hawk, and Peregrine received from their families. If they had families.

Still, they went through the ceremony, and Fallon snickered as Hawk and Peregrine graduated as Olag and Poppy. The names were too funny, and she intended to tease them about it the next time they all met up at the bar. Which was becoming a much more regular thing.

Actually, they'd probably meet up that night, to celebrate graduation.

She smiled, thinking about drinks, pretzel knots, and telling exaggerated stories loosely based on actual events.

Hawk specialized in those.

She smiled bigger, thinking of the years ahead, and the many, many times they'd probably repeat that experience.

THE LAZY DAYS of rest they had after championships and graduation felt like a reward for the fast pace Fallon had kept for the past three years. The campus emptied out gradually, until only a handful of students remained.

Then that tiny but highly appreciated respite was suddenly over.

It was time to move on to whatever came next.

OTS loomed, and she knew little of what that would be like. Unlike the academy, OTS didn't happen all in one place. They'd get their basic training in how to be an officer first, here on Earth. Then they'd begin duty rotations in various locations, in accordance with their specialties.

Most likely, there would be times when they'd separate to receive their own specialized training, then come together again as a team.

She didn't know. Her future was a big, exciting question mark. At least she knew that whatever came her way, she'd have a team to go back to. People who would keep growing to better understand her. They'd make a new sort of family.

Today, she had an entirely different mission.

"Are you sure?" She pushed a vial back and forth with her fingertip before Peregrine snatched it away. The vial had teensy little black bits that looked like a fine powder.

"Completely. Hawk says his guy knows what he's doing, and will keep his mouth shut." Peregrine's jaw was set.

Fallon looked from Hawk to Peregrine. Was she really going to let some tattoo artist put whatever Peregrine had invented into her skin?

Yeah. She was. She had to trust her teammates.

Off they went, taking a groundcar to the nearby city. Hawk's friend looked rough, with tattoos on every bit of visible skin except for his face. He had a scar that cut through one of his eyebrows, too.

His shop was clean, though. As clinically organized and spot-free as a hospital. She even smelled a disinfectant bite in the air.

Hawk nodded to her, assuring her that this guy was for real.

After taking a deep breath, she nodded. "Okay. I'll go first. Let's do this."

She felt no fear or doubt. She would prove her trust in her

teammates, and show them she'd put herself in front of anything for them.

She lay on a table and pulled up her shirt to expose her abdomen.

"Here." She pointed to the left of her navel.

The tattoo artist, who went by the name of Fam, shaved and cleaned her skin with the efficiency of a healthcare professional.

His expertise reassured her.

He picked up the dermal injector, checked it, then reached for the vial Peregrine had given him. It held a unique blend of ink and nano-transmitters.

"Here's the design." Peregrine set the infoboard on the table on Fam's other side.

He gave it a long look, then nodded. "What is it?"

The looping design looked vaguely like a clover leaf, but with more swirls. Peregrine had created it.

"Just a design based on ancient Atalan hieroglyphs." She shrugged. "We thought it was cool."

"I've seen a lot worse," Fam said.

Fallon got the feeling he was the kind of guy who rarely praised anything. But she liked the design. Peregrine had taken the words for *blood* and *bone*, interlinked them, and made them into a unique image.

It was a good thing she liked it, since it would now be inked on her body.

She didn't know if PAC command would approve of this, but they had no intention of telling anyone what the tattoos really were.

Peregrine had designed nano-transmitters that would be inserted into their skin. The tattoos would disguise them. On the outside, they'd be school friends who got matching tattoos to celebrate graduating the academy and beginning OTS.

On the inside, they'd have a way for them to always track one another, so long as they had a properly tuned receiver and were within range.

"I'm ready," Fam said. "Do you want an anesthetic?"

"No, I must foolishly gain the respect of my friends by taking the painful route." She wasn't lying.

Hawk guffawed and Raptor smiled, then said, "Scrap, that means I'll have to do it that way, too, or risk being seen as a wimp."

Hawk gave him a friendly but hard slap on the back. "Don't worry, frat boy. We already see you that way."

They all laughed, except Peregrine, who did her half-smile thing.

"Be still," Fam ordered.

Fallon stopped laughing.

After her, Raptor got his tattoo in the same place. Hawk opted to get his on the left side of his chest, while Peregrine chose her left shoulder blade.

"What do I owe you?" Hawk asked when they were done.

"A thousand cubics. Or you could hang onto the money and just owe me a favor."

Hawk grinned. "I'll pay the money. It'll be cheaper in the long run."

Funny how much more easily he smiled and laughed when in a place like this, away from the campus.

The academy must have been very, very hard on him. So far, he hadn't opened up about that. Maybe someday he would.

Hawk transferred the cubics via an infoboard, and they were done. "Should we go grab a drink? Blue Nine's just a few blocks that way." He jerked his thumb to the left.

"It's a little early," Peregrine observed. "We haven't even had dinner."

"So order some Bennite food delivered to us at Blue Nine. I'll spring for pretzel knots," Hawk suggested.

"I suppose that's all right." Peregrine flipped her ponytail back over her shoulder.

As they walked, Raptor joked, "Now that we have matching tattoos, we have to be best friends forever. We can go shopping together, do each other's hair, and snuggle while watching holo-vids."

Hawk closed his eyes in a long-suffering look of chagrin, slowly shaking his head from side to side. "Dude. No."

Fallon laughed. She loved Raptor's sense of humor. Though they'd graduated, they hadn't yet ended their romantic relationship. They'd need to, though. Soon.

Eventually.

Along the way, Peregrine handed them simple silver bracelets. "Here. Wear these at all times. They have the receivers in them. I'll show you how to use them later."

Emiko's was the smallest, and it fit her wrist just right.

Raptor put his on, shrugged, and let his arm fall to his side. "I'm stylish enough to make this work." He nodded toward Hawk. "Don't know about that guy, though."

Hawk smirked at him. "I have more style in my big toe than you do in your whole body."

He put on his bracelet, shook it at Raptor, and said, "Hah."

At Blue Nine, they drank, ate Bennite stew and pretzels, and talked. Then they drank and talked some more. They spent the rest of the day there, and on into the night. They didn't talk about their first lives or their feelings or their hopes and dreams. Mostly, they told impossible stories, made jokes, and laughed.

But they said what mattered. Without using the actual words, they told one another that they were a team, that they would look out for each other, and that they would face whatever came next together.

"Blood and bone!" Hawk said, raising his recently refilled mug.

The rest of them raised their glasses to his.

"Blood and bone!"

MESSAGE FROM THE AUTHOR

Thank you for reading!

If you enjoyed this story and can spare a minute or two to leave a review on Amazon, I'd be grateful. It makes a big difference.

If you're ready for more Chains of Command, check out *Blood and Bone*. Avian unit is headed to OTS, and there's bound to be trouble.

Be sure to visit www.ZenDiPietro.com and sign up for Zen's newsletter so you'll never miss a new release or sale. Stay tuned for more adventures!

I hope to hear from you!

In gratitude,
Zen DiPietro

ABOUT THE AUTHOR

Zen DiPietro is a lifelong bookworm, dreamer, and writer. Perhaps most importantly, a Browncoat Trekkie Whovian. Also red-haired, left-handed, and a vegetarian geek. Absolutely terrible at conforming. A recovering gamer, but we won't talk about that. Particular loves include badass heroines, British accents, and the smell of Band-Aids.

Visit Zen's website at www.ZenDiPietro.com.

Printed in Great Britain
by Amazon